VIRAGO
MODERN CLASSICS
710

Dorothea Tanning

Dorothea Tanning (1910–2012) was born in Galesburg, Illinois, and attended Knox College before moving to New York in the 1940s. There she began exhibiting at the Julien Levy Gallery, becoming known for her very personal and powerful surrealist paintings. In New York she met and married Max Ernst, moving with him to Arizona in the mid '40s, and then to France in the mid '50s. Two decades later, after Ernst's death, Tanning returned to New York, where she embarked upon a new and ambitious series of paintings, increasing both the scale and the scope of her work. Her work is included in collections at the Tate Gallery, the Georges Pompidou Centre, the Museum of Modern Art, New York, and the Menil Collection, Houston. Tanning published her only novel, *Chasm: A Weekend*, when she was ninety-four. She also wrote a memoir and two collections of poetry.

CHASM

A Weekend

Dorothea Tanning

VIRAGO

This paperback edition published in 2019 by Virago Press
First published in Great Britain in 2004 by Virago Press

5 7 9 10 8 6 4

A CIP catalogue record for this book
is available from the British Library.

ISBN 978-0-349-01262-9

Typeset in Goudy by M Rules
Printed and bound in Great Britain by
Clays Ltd, Elcograf S.p.A.

Papers used by Virago are from well-managed forests
and other responsible sources.

Virago Press
An imprint of
Little, Brown Book Group
Carmelite House
50 Victoria Embankment
London EC4Y ODZ

An Hachette UK Company
www.hachette.co.uk

www.virago.co.uk

Destina Descending

(chronology)

In 1682, Destina Kirby, of Portsmouth, England, married a seaman, Tray Thomas, first mate of the *Georgic*, plying the seas between England and the New World. On its next voyage, she joined him. As a pair they settled in Maine but soon moved to Massachusetts. A daughter was named for her mother, Thomas being so much in love as to be unwilling to admit that any other name existed; indeed, he declared that no female descendant of theirs should ever be called otherwise. Not to dwell overlong on their life in Naumkeag, it may be noted that, Thomas continuing in his profession, the two Destinas were much alone for long periods, and after three years, due to a tragedy at sea in which Thomas was drowned, the condition became permanent. The mother, dreamy and introspective, often whiled away the long evening hours after her little girl was asleep in writing verses always addressed to a 'you'. These she kept locked away; but they were later ferreted out during her trial for witchcraft, and were declared by her judges to be addressed to the devil himself. Her poems, her much envied beauty and the fire opal (a souvenir from Thomas's exotic travels) were enough to send her to the flames in the 1692 witch hunt. The kindness of a neighbor was responsible for the rescue of the little girl, that lady having run to the schoolhouse, taken Destina, and brought her to the inn. There a ragged caravan was on the point of leaving and the bewildered child was thrust into it without a word as it rolled away. She was seven years old.

Destina Thomas's is a long story that must be abridged here. Enough to say that at age fifteen she was employed as a seamstress and wardrobe mistress for the family of Simon Bentby, a chief justice in Boston. His was a rather grand household: a large family of some fashion, principally three elegant daughters and a son, Josiah, for whom elegance meant nothing at all. In fact his sighs were reserved for Destina Thomas whose beauty so far eclipsed that of his sisters that despite her excellent work with needle and thread the young ladies conspired to have her relieved of her employment. She was nineteen years old.

In 1707, Destina Thomas finally married Josiah Bentby, but shortly after, died in childbirth. Their child, Destina, born 1708, could not adequately console her heartbroken father, who after several years remarried, albeit so disastrously that he took sail from Boston one day with his seven-year-old daughter for London. As a London beauty, Destina Bentby was in no hurry to marry, but on reaching the age of twenty-seven she finally accepted what was then the only life available to a decent woman.

In 1735, therefore, she married the Rt. Hon. Lord Sevenish of Sussex, and, as Lady Destina, presided uneventfully over a country estate with her family of two sons and their much younger sister, Destina (born 1750), who, as will be seen, did not come to appreciate the halls and gardens of Sussex. In 1766, she eloped to Paris with a poor relative, John Lansing, who believed himself to be an artist. Pursued by an agent of the infuriated Lord Sevenish, they fled with their two-year-old Destina (born 1767) to Rome. There, Lansing found employment as assistant in a painter's atelier, while his wife and, later, his daughter, served as artist's models. The younger Destina, with her handsome face and truly beautiful body, became a favorite subject for the sculptors of the day; it was even rumored that she was the model for Canova's *Hebe* figures and the celebrated *Psyche*.

In 1797, Destina Lansing, weary of adventures, married a Roman politician, Carlo di Cola, member of the *consulta straordinaria*. She had become something of a figure in the salons of artist and nobleman alike. Her daughter, Destina (born 1807), like her grandmother Sevenish, preferred the former.

In 1830, Destina di Cola married an impecunious actor

(name unknown), who, after a year, left with his *commedia* troupe and forgot to return. Her equally headstrong daughter (born 1832) was, in her turn, captivated by a Captain Converse, an American explorer whose El Dorado was simply the far west of America, which he declared to be his imminent destination.

In 1857, Destina di Cola, bewitched not only by the captain but by his stories about the world beyond Europe and even New England, married her American. She then used her influence to help raise the funds they would need for their adventure, and together they crossed sea and land, arriving miraculously in territory wrested from Mexican control in 1848, a southern outpost of California. Only one child, a girl called Destina (or Dessie, by her father), was born (1867) to this couple who battled the wilderness, developing a toughness undreamed-of back in Rome. Captain Converse lost no time in staking his claim to lands as barren as they were vast. Water was eventually discovered nearby, and after seventeen years the ranch had so prospered that Dessie was sent, over the objections of the Captain, to Italy for an education that her mother felt was not to be had at home.

In 1887, Destina Converse was married to Vittorio di Vicini, descendant of a once-great family of Florence, long since strangers to a bank account. His *palazzo* of phantom plumbing, leaky roofs and peeling plaster gave her what her father, the captain, would have called 'the creeps'.

She vowed that her own daughter (born in 1890) would fare better.

In 1917, after two unsuitable engagements, Destina di Vicini was married off to the Austro-Italian Baron Heinrich von Schönwald. Their only child, a daughter (the baron had fully expected a son), was born in 1920 and betrothed at birth, as part of some merger, to the son, already age twelve, of a prestigious family of neighboring industrialists.

Dismayed by their luxuriously vapid life and appalled at her husband's gross self-interest, the baroness, in a plot as picturesque – and as dangerous – as it was successful, decamped with her child to America and the distant ranch which, though empty (her grandparents had died), seemed to be waiting for them. Or so felt the Baroness Destina as she drew in a deep breath of crystal desert air.

In 1937, her adored daughter Destina, now seventeen, was literally abducted by emissaries of her father, Baron Heinrich, and brought back to his villa. There, an almost immediate disappointment turned to boredom and regret. The omnipresence of Fascism seemed not to disturb the baron who, in fact, didn't appear to mind it at all. What had been represented to the girl Destina as a more civilized lifestyle struck her as sinister and unreal; an independent spirit had been forged in her desert home. Prevented by her utter powerlessness from escaping back to her mother and her beloved dunes she often roamed the countryside.

An idyll with a young man of the village on leave from the army resulted in a 'situation' intolerable to her grand family, and the disgusted Baron in a hasty arrangement married her off to an acquaintance. This man was Raoul Meridian. Her baby girl, born the following spring (1941) and named Destina, would carry his name while he set out, alone, to claim and inhabit his wife's American ranch, where he was obliged to endure the presence of her mother as part of the bargain. The baroness waited for years in the old ranch house for her daughter's return; Meridian always finding some reason to delay her arrival. During this time he was engaged in building the strange edifice he professed to be for her reception. Seventeen years passed in this way, as Windcote was born.

Returning to Europe on one of his always mysterious errands he learned that his wife had died and her bereft daughter, aged seventeen, was with child, father unknown. He did not inquire, he asked no questions – he offered marriage. What in the eyes of the world would have been a shocking admission was avoided by his carrying her off to Windcote, where, as we will see, having borne her child (1958), a daughter, she soon ends her life. That child is Destina Meridian, with whom the reader is about to become acquainted.

I

Few travelers ever see the buildings of Windcote. The ranch, despite its vast size, is ringed with fence, and two cattleguards must be crossed to enter the property. After that, for several miles of punishing washboard road there is still nothing but dust and cactus. Then, abruptly, the house is there, as shocking as a fallen meteor. Ponderous, tall, defiant and truly alien, it nicks the desert like a weapon.

Clearly there is no gentle intimacy for Windcote, no cradling by red earth for this anachronism, this jumbled pile of wood and stone, this uneasy amalgamation of architectural whims. Its lines shimmer uncertainly in the waning daylight of a Friday afternoon. Its shadowed side has a crouching expression in spite of its three stories piled one on the other, thrust into the startled space between earth and sky, an uncertain mass.

The gazer looks in vain for some clue to the builder's intention. Could the big, vaguely Byzantine entrance reached by wings of gray stone stairs lead to cheerful murmur, smiling welcome? Could the little belvedere, hung with mad care on the west façade above a leaded window, be anything but a gratuity, a wart, a fragment of baby-talk clinging to the ear? Had the hand of the architect been ground to meat before he grasped the crayon? Questions that wither in the desert glare while the house looms, nerveless and heavy, born of itself. On its massive façade the evening's red rays seem to sear instead of caress, and on the two round towers, with their mullioned windows, the departing sun casts its daily crimson frown of repudiation. Surely Windcote, its very name a masquerade, can only have sprung full-blown from some conjurer's chant; so it must one day vanish, leaving perhaps for one wild instant a puff of black smoke on the scorched sand.

In a dormer room on the top floor of the house stands Nelly, the 'governess', gazing at her reflection in a mirror on the wall. She has pulled up her dark cotton skirt and a shabby ruffled petticoat so that her stomach is bare; holding the clothes under her chin she turns her body's profile to the glass. The room, with its one window and corner closet, is small and cramped. In order to see her stomach's contour in the spotted glass Nelly is obliged to stand squeezed and contorted between the narrow bed and an immense wardrobe trunk. Even so it is almost impossible to see into the mirror, for the trunk as well as nearly every other flat surface is piled high with what Nelly calls her 'finds' – pieces of gnarled and weathered juniper wood. These knotted gray objects lie in tangled heaps in the corners, on the windowsill, the one chair, everywhere, even on the bed, where there is hardly room to lie down. They dominate the tiny room, give it an air of arrested agony, as if, in an awful moment, a burst of conjuration, Nelly's fetishes might throw off their spell to fulfill some ugly destiny. Yet she loves them; to her it is all very pretty and she is happy here.

When she came to Windcote it was assumed that she would share the comfortable apartments of her little charge, the daughter of the house. She refused. Oh no. Give her a room of her own, a private room, no matter how small or humble. And as she was not really a servant but had come as companion and governess, her request was granted. No one else ever enters the room. Nelly herself carries the key hidden on a cord under her skirt – a useless precaution since no one has ever shown the least interest in it.

'I wonder,' murmurs Nelly, her gaze searching the darkening glass, 'I wonder if it really is any bigger. Could it be just imagination? Yes, I think it is – being inclined as I am to imagine things, no matter what. Still, I wonder . . . '

She passes her hand over her naked stomach in a dreamy circular movement, staring meanwhile at the cluttered trunk top with her soft expressionless eyes. Absent, almost sleepy, she pulls from the mass on the trunk a silvery root in the shape of a double spiral. Holding it above her head she sways gently and begins to sing:

Is it any wonder that I wonder . . .
If you're wond'ring dear about me . . .

Seizing a nail from a china tray, she pulls off a shoe and begins to pound the nail into almost the only blank space on the wall, hangs the dead root on the nail, and sinks in rapt admiration on the edge of the bed. She is perfectly square; her square jawline, wide mouth and flat, level nose correspond like a full square moon with the horizon of her shoulders, the folded arms, the plateau of her wide-set knees.

Far away someone is ringing a bell. Slowly Nelly stands up and opens the top bureau drawer. Rummaging among its contents she finds a bag of pale green nougats. Once neat cubes, they are now softened and glued together by the heat, but she twists one off and puts it in her mouth, then, feeling for her key, she leaves the room, locks the door, and walks in a soft, straight line to the stairs.

I wonder, I wonder
Is it any wonder that I wonder . . .

Down in the dining room, a little girl sits at the head of a long table completely laid for a dining party of eight. Beyond the heavily draped windows evening spreads reddishly over the desert, ennobling even the two mules being driven toward a small arroyo. The desert at this time of day,

10

so indulgent in its rosiness, gently cradles the two mules and stains with pink light the face of the driver who steps expertly between the cactus spines.

Here, in the big shadowy room with its carved pilasters, crystal sconces, ponderous sideboards and leather-backed chairs the little girl is, for her part, superbly unaware of the evening outside, the arroyo, the mules, the dusty Mexican driver. Pretty sunsets interest her not at all; for her the desert is something else, its reality for her alone. She sits motionless, and in the tall chair looks absurdly doll-like. Her dainty slippers, the bare pink arms, the very small drooping mouth, all combine in a kind of photo-album artifice, so that glancing into the room with its deepening shadows and sensing some perverse mise-en-scène in the charming vision there, one might almost be disappointed at seeing the little person actually close her eyes.

Yet this is what she presently does. She closes her eyes for several moments, as if waiting for something to appear, something she has willed to appear on the table. The room perceptibly darkens, it has grown late. The furniture, glassware, silver – all gleam in an iridescent gloom where surfaces slyly shift and merge. Only the little figure remains clear and fixed in the carved chair. Her pale skin and white dress light up the beating dimness like phosphorus. From her right hand clenched before her on the table oozes a viscous fluid. It bubbles up between her fingers and spins out thickly on the tablecloth. She opens her eyes, looks at the object in her hand, then stiffens at the sound of a voice from the doorway.

'Desta, are you there?'

Down the length of the room comes Nelly, peering through the gloom. She stumbles on a protruding chair, thrusts it away with her hip, mutters a weary 'damn!' under her breath and stops to set it right. She sees the little girl sitting in her aura of whiteness.

'Oh there you are, Dessie, why didn't you answer? It's late, time to go upstairs. Come on. We're going up now.'

The girl smiles at her but doesn't move.

'You crazy kid,' Nelly goes on, 'why are you sitting here, anyway?' She gazes along the splendidly laid table. 'Let's go, they'll all be coming in soon. Besides, we have to' – she pauses and stares – 'What's that stuff in your hand?'

At this the child snatches her hand from the table. 'Go away.'

Nelly must have heard these words before. Not at all surprised, her bland, square face is even matter-of-fact while she pulls at the little girl's shoulder. 'Really, Desta, you can't stay here. We're not supposed to be here at all, you know that. Now come on . . .'

Turning her face toward the far left corner of the room, the child smiles again, 'Do I have to, Papa?' she inquires nicely.

There is a faint rustling of draperies at one of the long windows. Squinting in the direction of the child's gaze,

Nelly makes out a blurred form between the window and a low credenza. Presently an indolent man's voice replies.

'Why yes, I suppose so. Yes, of course,' and he laughs quietly.

Sliding down from the chair, the little girl holds a clenched hand to her chest and with the other takes that of her governess. They walk toward the window, and as they draw near, the blurred form becomes a man, his ponderous form bent over a package lying across his knees. The package is long and narrow, something rolled, and from one end droops a skein of yellow hair. The little girl comes near, moves her hand behind her back, and lifts her face to his.

He kisses her lightly on the cheek. 'Goodnight, Destina.'

She gazes for a moment into his heavy face. 'Good night then, Papa.'

When they have reached the door he calls to Nelly. She walks back to his chair; he speaks without looking up. 'You will spend the evening alone or with Destina. Try to get some control over yourself. Try to remember that I am Meridian, your employer, and I will be very taken up until tomorrow. Do you understand?'

She turns without answering and, dragging her feet, leaves the room.

On the tablecloth the stains of fluid have turned a ruddy brown. The house begins to fill with evening sounds. By the window the man, Raoul Meridian, bends his head and unwraps the package, revealing a thick fall of pale hair.

13

With shaking shoulders and something like the sound of sobbing, he strains it against his face.

Mounting the stairs with Destina, Nelly was half conscious of a puzzlement tickling the back of her neck. She saw again the table laid for eight, not four as it had been last evening. She and Destina always checked weekend arrivals from the window; watching cars roll up on the gravel below was a game easy to play. Yesterday there were just three: Ritter – oh, she knew *him*; and later a young man and a girl, the tops of their heads dark and blond. But then Carmela, with an important look, came up to tell her, 'The boss says "Tell Miss Nelly I'll be busy all evening."' That old bat Carmela with her wise looks . . . Then later, much later, she saw that same young man alone outside. Hey, where was his girlfriend? Or wife maybe? What was he doing out there alone, pacing back and forth, not even looking up? Oh, who cares, she had told herself. That was yesterday. Yesterday was over and good riddance. Tonight would be as usual. But no. Tonight would not be as usual either. He had just said so. She was frowning. What's going on anyway?

And Destina? If, climbing the stairs, she was now as docile as a rag doll it was simply that she knew it was easier that way, easier to fool Nelly, easier to keep her own rendezvous. For outside in the canyon waited her only understanding of reality. Borne along as she was by her all-encompassing secret, she saw this stair, this Nelly and, yes, this Papa as dubious if not make-believe.

Possibly Meridian was aware of her remoteness or saw its signs, but the fact is that he hardly noticed Destina. To him she was not the smallest part of the world that contained him and his guests.

Although devoted to certain social mores, this Meridian, master of Windcote, liked everyone there, especially the women, to break the rules for dinner attire. His own body without grace, he had long since realized that the dry black and white reduced it to anonymity and gave him an unfinished look, as if sculpted in a hurry. He wore his velvets and brocades at all times of the year, even in summer when beads of sweat stood like glitter on his face, without for a moment disturbing the élan of his pose; detached, sultanic, undeniably effective. Effective, that is, if one were to judge by some of his guests, who, for their own separate reasons as well as his, made variously successful efforts to harmonize with, if not to rival, his eccentric dress.

He was a monument of puzzling freakishness to many, including his employees, who saw in him a certain dire personification of malignant forces, while closing their eyes and minds to them for the sake of their salaries. One or two were rather grandly paid, in fact, for sometimes trivial and undemanding work, such as deliveries of heavy packets on horseback: a trek through trailless sierras with a scraggy cabin at its end; or a service station and cafe, wind-lashed and unnamed, in the mesquite country behind the range to the east. Whatever they thought of these and others of their instructions, they did not ask questions; it was part of the 'no nonsensical prying' understanding with the boss – a firm requirement that if flouted could have a nasty, if not violent, mishap in store for the very accident-prone worker. They may have wondered, in their way, what gasp of nature could have produced so fungoid a growth of glistening flesh. In imitation of human bulk he sat on his horse or in his princely chair, sardonic behind an air of benevolent ease. It was said of him (the gossip of his guests – as always, the best source) that he had left his Florentine *palazzo* in a hurry after the Great War, something about difficulties with the *securita*. Rumors abounded without anything appearing clearly, just as on a blurred photograph conjecture must replace outline.

On immigration papers he gave his birthplace as Bratesca, a tiny backwater on the Black Sea too small to be found on a common atlas. Once, in a tedious questionnaire episode it was revealed that his father, after the family removed as far west as Zagreb, had continued farther into Europe, finding work in the experimental laboratories of a Krupps branch somewhere in the Austrian Alps. (Village inhabitants hearing an occasional explosion suspected nothing unusual, accustomed as they were to reverberations of frequent avalanches.) There he apprenticed his son to a small business in prosthetic appliances destined for the sick, maimed or elderly – that is, for those who could afford them. These devices, painstakingly executed and articulated in leather, steel, and rubber, became ever more ingenious, as new means and materials presented new possibilities. To his intimates Meridian (he had traded the name for his own unpronounceable one) loved to point out that while his father was working on machines that, properly aimed, could blow a victim into six equal fragments – head, arms, legs, and torso, like pieces of ancient sculpture found in art museums – his boss was laboring to provide them with artificial ones.

In any case, the apprenticeship had served him well. Having tasted from early childhood the pleasures of self-gratification, he had never felt any need to complicate his simple onanistic life by engaging with another, he had never gazed longingly at a human being or dreamed of holding one in his arms. Nevertheless, his hitherto so adequate masturbatory interludes had begun to pall, his needs to grow more sophisticated.

He began experimenting with the same materials he had learned to manipulate in the shop, but with different possibilities of articulation. He persisted in calling them games, these elegant devices that soon found a vast shadowy network of demand on five continents and made his fortune. Moreover, along with the solid income from filling orders, there was, as if for the taking, the attendant sideline of blackmail. This activity, which had secured for him all sorts of possessions from simple money to entire estates, one of them being the Italian *palazzo* that preceded his California domain – a windfall, by the way, that required from him nothing more than a marriage certificate.

It was all so graceful. And his removal to this desert domain had not at all interrupted certain of his activities about which even foggier rumors drifted. There were frequent visits to Windcote by men somehow like himself: ponderous and silent, seemingly unacquainted with the amenities. They arrived in tightly closed cars, sometimes even in vans that had a rather armored look. Except for the evening meal, taken together by those who were in the house, the hours of the day and often enough those of the night as well were passed by these visitors with Meridian behind his locked door. It was also rumored that behind his locked door there were other doors firmly bolted.

He had never been known to sit on the terrace. He had never been seen in the greenhouse – to the gardener's relief, incidentally, for there was an absurd but persistent story of how a flower had once visibly wilted in his hand; the kind of story that locals take to their hearts with awe and even belief. In the ten off and on years that Meridian had spent at Windcote numerous legends, always of this same uneasy nature, had sprung up about him. He was one of those people whom one cannot imagine ever having been an infant but to have hatched, in response to an oracular command accompanied by lightning, earthquake and tidal wave, from some monstrous egg. As such he dragged his destiny after him. Or was he dragged by it instead?

Of his local tenancy little had ever been mentioned. The older Indians, an elderly woman living down in an adobe ranch house by the wash, and a half-mad prospector tolerated by Meridian on the vast premises – he remembered perhaps too much for the boss's comfort – remembered their coming: the strangely aged, heavy man bringing with him, after a long absence, a very young girl who, except for her round belly, was as wraithlike as the man was imposing. No one bothered to inform the baroness – the situation was messy enough, deemed Meridian, who at the same time was wondering how to restore his sovereign solitude. He had not long to wait. The heartbroken girl bore her child, whom she named Destina, drank some sort of lethal poison, and died in convulsions. Coroners, undertakers and, later, papers to sign. Soon it was if she had never been there except for the baby Destina, nursed by servants until Nelly's arrival.

In this fifty-thousand-acre desert waste, where the only water came from a well near Manzanita Wash – and the annual downpour that within hours evaporated – Raoul Meridian's presence was like a failed collage, incongruous, inept. He knew this, and didn't mind – he had dealt with incongruities before. But a someone, an annoyance, pesky, buzzing at the bottom of his wine glass, subject of the nasty clause in those papers, was also there – the woman down in the sprawl of her old ranch house by the creek. Oh, not that the ranch was hers, not one acre of it. All of that had been taken care of, everything signed by his wife before she died. But her grandmother – yes, that's who she was – would be allowed to stay as long as she lived. So on occasion he would even invite her in to participate in his evenings as an eccentric old family member, a harmless addition to the décor and, as a baroness, a proof of his own authenticity.

On the surface, life at Windcote, gracious and leisurely as it was, intrigued everyone who came there. Its rakish style, combined with its proximity to raw wilderness, gave even the most entrenched pragmatist a tiny frisson of adventure. And the eccentricities of its master, far from provoking criticism, made others sometimes wonder if they had been missing something. Though not actually asking for it, as already mentioned, he liked his guests to compete with his own sartorial cheek, with the result that his dinner parties, when everyone was on hand, generally resembled failed Halloweens. No exception was this evening, when eight people came down to dinner. Eight people. For Meridian there was only one, a guest, Nadine Coussay. She was radiance itself with her cap of cropped pale hair – he almost closed his eyes, thinking of the long strands cut that very afternoon, for *him*. He had found the only candidate he could contemplate for the extravagance waiting in the laboratory. All the years spent on experiment – for what were creatures like Nelly, or the others, but virtual affronts to his ingenuity – were only a long prologue to this night and its event. But was he so certain of what that event might be? Had he not known other beauties in his life? From what has already been revealed it isn't easy to understand how Meridian could be captivated by a Nadine, however beautiful. In view of his history and his skewed sexuality there seemed no reason for such a capitulation before mere feminine beauty. But if the question persists, and if the asker is willing to venture into darker territory, to descend deeper into the miasma of a mind so warped by its own ingenious perversities that there could be no surprise at his whims, then any reason would do. To those watching he was simply infatuated. Understandably: older man, beautiful girl. Or so they thought. His reason, however, if reason can serve as a word here, was far from infatuation. It was capture. Toward what ends? Tonight will answer that, he would have replied.

2

If anyone had reminded Nadine Coussay that she came from a lordly and ancient line of French knights and ladies she would have listened with a shrug. What she knew for sure was that everything came to her with little effort on her part and that the past, whatever that was, had nothing to do with her; for indeed she was turned, almost belligerently, toward its opposite – *l'avenir*, her father would have called it. He was one of those dreamers who, like his father and grandfather and the family before them, had long since forgotten the names Artois, Hainault, d'Aunay, Coucy; names they had no use for, living as they did since before remembered time, like an endangered species, in the Attacapan swampland of Louisiana. With his sleepy government job, his front-porch cronies, and the swaying feathery trees to fan him he saw no reason to interrogate either the *passé* or the *avenir*. His pretty motherless daughter thought only of escape. Upon reaching puberty, and bored to death with her quaint neighbors and their stubborn French jargon, she wangled admittance to a distant parochial school from which, after a sketchy education in things like cooking and embroidery rather than the classics and sciences, it was easy to let her by now remarkable beauty lead her, as entranced as a sleepwalker, to California.

There things happened. There were people, other kinds of people. Wherever she went – and she went a great deal – they gaped at her with that sudden silence and intake of breath that marks the tiny moment experienced at the sight of beauty. Even her speech had a bell-like roundness gilded with the merest hint of an accent – Acadian? Southern? It was like a cook's tantalizing secret that the diner tries vainly to identify. Because of this something every word she uttered sounded as if it had never been said before.

Unconsciously hooked on homage as on some drug, Nadine went on with her aimless round of events, ever confident of a future that would be played out some day soon in very different surroundings. It may have been this conviction that gave her the baffled, absent air so contrasted with the usual party animation of everyone else. She was thus seen as positively ethereal.

She deeply believed that she loved nature. Nature, like that. Nature outside of the cities. She would look around at her pleasant rooms with a sigh of disdain (and with not a thought of her daddy's regular checks that paid for them). Even the big blue sky and silvery pepper tree outside the window had nothing in common with the nature composed of tangled forests, sandblown deserts, waterfalls, mountain peaks, exotic animals and birds that decorated her thoughts, and where she was the only human presence (with possible guides). Mildly fearsome and highly colored, her view of nature was reverent and global, save that it did not include humans or pets. There were times when despite her own pesky category – 'humanoid' was her favorite word for it – she felt close to something, the wilderness, its mystery, its grandeur, even its implacable plan for herself. That plan, she was sure, saw her trekking through jungles or wadis, feeling their fastnesses penetrate her being and their dangers justify her daring.

In her closet there was not even one party dress of the sort that every young beauty dotes on. Her only dress was legendary: black, one of those garments called a sheath that is yearly presented as the latest mode and, in this case, with the added impression of something tired but serviceable, like the Sicilian peasant woman's perpetual black. So without even a strand of pearls she was always the most oddly garbed at any event, her black cloth no more than a concession to cover nakedness. She called herself an explorer, an adaptable term for Nadine, and very loosely defined, although her closet contained the proof, if anyone had wanted it: safari garments for the desert, anorak and clogs for mountain climbing, windbreakers, boots, camp gear, all the wistful never-used paraphernalia of someone who expects to brave the elements. But if that someone cannot live a day without the hour before the mirror, cannot neglect her glorious gift?

Because Nadine would never wear these things. And it was her simple, perfect beauty that enslaved her days, clogged her mind, and kept her locked into the foolish imitation of luxury that prevailed around her. When she looked at her face in the glass she was overcome by a sort of awed beatitude that stayed with her as she walked away and for hours afterward hindered the pursuit of any coherent thought. Powerful, insidious beauty was her burden, as heavy as an infirmity. Deft, slashing, it had separated her from the world of ordinary mortals and thrust her into a freakish position of anomaly. Even back in school, at seventeen, already trapped in her lonely little web of perfection, inexplicably moving apart from the others, she was mostly thoughtful and patient, as if sitting on a faraway station platform waiting for the train that took so long to appear.

There could be no describing Nadine by simple enumeration of her features – nose straight, skin white, eyes blue, hair long and yellow; nor by inclination, for every girl at seventeen has begun to look into that looming landscape of personal challenge. But when Nadine peered ahead she couldn't see anything. No matter. The future was not in this present. There was time; and plenty of that for asking questions. For now, there wasn't much to do. Everything but existing was done for her as she advanced more and more knowingly into the world. Meanwhile there were always parties, appointments, photo shoots, appearances, all arranged. She was a Hollywood familiar. Her wonderful face drifted in and out of studios and drawing rooms. A necessary vision, even a prophecy. If one had seen Nadine Coussay somewhere that day, one was saved, it wasn't clear from what. And the question was tantalizing: how could anyone so entrance her world and yet remain so radiantly apart; here in the center of filmmaking, with its intensities, its ambitions, its mystique?

Nadine did not act. It had of course been offered, even several times, by various studios, always with the gentlest indulgence and encouragement. But there was no spark. She saw no reason to try. No, she would wait for her adventure, her wilderness, and there was time like a long rainbow of a scarf undulating before her. Clearly, it was only a matter of time.

So while a man at a party sat on a patio with her, telling of his life at Windcote, the desert repair he had created only a two-hour drive from the city, she listened, and questioned, and glowed with pleasure. After half an hour he asked her to come out to Windcote on the next Friday afternoon. There would be a few friends. One could ride, explore the Indian ruins nearby ... Nadine caught at the words with deep excitement. She struck out. Her head swam with visions. She might have been Europa on the Bull, Jane in the canopy, Susan under Kilimanjaro. Then she remembered Albert. Well, it was all so tedious and confusing. She would have to explain. So she said she had a fiancé. That was her word: fiancé.

The man beside her was Raoul Meridian, his imposing hulk silhouetted against the light from the house. Nadine smiled her famous smile. When she mentioned a fiancé Meridian sat back and answered smoothly, 'By all means, bring him along. By all means. I'll be very glad to meet him,' and added urgently, 'He's sure to be special if he's yours.'

'Not mine yet,' Nadine smiled again, 'but a friend, and we're engaged.'

'Friend or enemy,' said Meridian, looking hard into her face, 'let us have him.'

She accepted then. It was utterly tempting. For what was tempting Nadine without her conscious naming of it had nothing to do with the healthy explorer's relation to nature and its marvels but another kind of experience – in her words, the unknown. This unknown of hers had immediately made itself felt in the man sitting beside her, so different from anyone she knew. Albert, gentle Albert, and his place in her life was fading almost to transparency by comparison. She was restless, confused. Was Albert really what she wanted?

Meridian was outlining directions and arrangements for the two-day weekend stay, and after the *au revoirs* she turned and walked into the house. A strange man, thought Nadine, not quite knowing whether she was perplexed or intrigued but preferring the latter. And Windcote. It sounded just right.

All that remained was to persuade Albert. That he would agree to go as readily as she had was unlikely. She geared herself to win him over.

Late that evening as they lay in bed she drew away from his side and rolled on her back, arms behind her head, with just a slight thrust of the hip that, consciously or not, achieved grace. She was thinking hard, not about Albert but about needing to talk to him. Her long pale hair flowed over the pillow toward his face and smelled, he told himself, like young vines. It was the first thing he had felt upon seeing her: she was a plant. Now, as his eyes followed the lines of this body beside him in all their sinuous meanders, as he kept his hands from her hair so as not to disturb the pose, he too was thinking and believing that he was in love.

Nadine reached down to pull up the sheet. It was an unfamiliar gesture that Albert idly noticed. And was followed by an announcement.

'We're invited to a house party.'

'Who we?'

'You and me. Way out in the desert. A place called Windcote,' said Nadine, very fast. 'A person I met this afternoon at that reception—'

'What are you talking about?' broke in Albert, amazed.

'But I just told you. Meridian. That's his name. He has

this spread out near the border. It's an easy two-hour drive. He asked me for next weekend. I told him about you and he said to bring you along.'

'Really.' A pause. 'I'm not the sort of man who's brought along.' He turned away to pick up his watch and put it on. Nadine sat up.

'You don't understand. He wants to meet you,' and added nicely, 'After all, we *are* engaged.'

Albert winced. That word. Of course he was engaged. To be married. That was how Nadine saw it, how it had to be. A game he would play, at least novel, something – he thought grimly – that would have appealed to the family. Oh no, this must not even be thought of, must not shadow his present role – he would see to that.

Albert's family, which he abhorred, was an extended one by the name of Exodus. Exodus uncles, aunts and cousins abounded. All had cut their teeth on silver spoons or, more correctly, diamond ones – two centuries of Exodus know-how having long dominated the world diamond market from their plush headquarters in Antwerp, Johannesburg, and lately, New York. They were proud, quiet, laconic, and walked carefully, as if the weight of their grandeur had made them somehow fearful. For the birth of Albert, third child, first son of Jan Exodus, there had been some discreet rejoicing, even though his appearance had cost his mother her life; mothers, while not exactly expendable in this milieu, could be replaced, as his was after a respectful interval. Except for a sister (another had died in infancy) always away somewhere, the boy grew up surrounded by people he hardly knew but who were nevertheless poised to receive him into the corporate fold upon his graduation from college. That is, until his nineteenth year, when they became fretful about his excesses, his scrapes, his galling rebellion. Moreover it was becoming costly. So the chair he was to occupy at board meetings remained empty – as if he had died. The truth was that he simply didn't want to sit in it.

A day came when he was legally turned loose, cut off from family and fortune with a modest allowance to support a modest lifestyle, and keep him quiet. They hoped he would stay away. For Albert it was a day of release. Free of 'tribal coercion', he pursued his chimera where it led: whether into pleasure or pain, sunny or dark places, and like Nadine, he couldn't find himself anywhere. Unlike her, however, he didn't have any dreams, however frail, to deaden the ache.

Nadine was watching him, waiting, preparing to be offended. He took some time to put on and set his watch and to examine his present mood. Why not give in to the moment, the easy way? After all, she had thrown in her lot with him, a drifter like herself, when another might have been chosen, someone who could take proper care of this very fragile being. He remembered how it had charmed him to think of his love for her, and surely it was charming the way she had liked him at once, had signed up for him. She didn't mind his slouch, his very unfashionable pointed beard, his periods of silence. He was so thin that there seemed to be no isolating material between the bones and the cloth. 'I like bones,' she had said. It was that simple.

'Yes,' he murmured.

'Well, "yes" what? Yes we're engaged or yes you'll go?'

He laughed then. 'Yes.'

'So you'll come with me?'

'Put that way I'd be a cad not to.'

Nadine, bridling, 'That's not an answer. Not a real one anyway. But don't you see? It's an experience. A chance to be close to nature, desert nature.'

Albert felt that he had been very close to nature all evening.

'How long will you stay?' he asked. She said just two days. 'There'll be others. You'll enjoy it. Really.'

'I'll enjoy it,' he repeated after her. He lay quiet in the sights and smells of their evening, the patio lights through the blinds striping Nadine's body from forehead to knees, the four walls holding them both in their cool embrace, their peace. This was all Albert wanted. Why would it not stay, like a picture on the wall, a treasure? Was this to be another bitter wind, another hollow tunnel? There had been so many. Oh, he knew there were no radiant answers, that he would always founder. He was no dreamer – dream was a narrow escape hatch that he simply did not fit. And the present liaison was no dream in any case. The personal chasm that yawned between him and this woman was unfathomable; he knew that too. But the idea of courtliness pleased him, he was Roland, he was Aucassin, a knight errant – if just a little cynical, only slightly fake. And, after all, how agreeable it was to have decisions made for him, like suits or soufflés. The thought made him smile. Why be so grave, why the melancholy? But it pervaded the moment, airless and brown, with the familiar sense of *déjà vécu*.

Come. Get hold of yourself, Albert. Even if there is nothing in store but boredom, stony, pulverizing boredom. Two days? Two fragments of present and future, two uncertainties to be dealt with, two beings, one of them seeing enough in this outlandish picture to commence fulfilling a few of her flimsy desires, the other bracing himself for compliance.

3

Such thoughts might have occurred to Albert as, with Nadine, he approached the place where they were to spend two days. Instead of the expected ranch house with its rambling, offhand invitation, this very odd prospect rose before them. They arrived at sundown, silent and tired after the three- (not two-) hour drive. Ochre dust and tumbleweed had not lightened Albert's mood. The harsh monotony of the road was tiring and oppressive. He would not have confessed to apprehension but he felt will-less and melancholy. Nor was he at all moved to marvel, as did Nadine, at the blazing dunes seen along the way. Finally, at sight of Windcote, when it was perfectly clear that they had arrived, he turned to Nadine. 'I don't believe this,' he said, and to himself, 'Now we are complete.'

'Come on,' said the girl in her firm girl's voice. 'Look over there, those hills. That must be where the Indian ruins are. You can ride. Horses for everyone, he told me . . . '

In the hall they were met by a young Mexican houseman in sneakers, jeans and velvet blouse, who took the valise (they had only one) and said, 'You follow, please,' turning to the wide staircase. They both hesitated. 'Come,' he said and smiled, 'the boss is outside, on horse. He see you later.'

Upstairs, through a winding hallway and a door, 'This one for the miss.'

It was one of those moments. Albert stopped, frowning. An intention rose before him, as blinding as surgery. Muffled, it leaned over them with quiet care as Nadine shook his arm. 'What did you expect, silly? Any other way would be, well, vulgar. After all ... ' She walked to a window. 'Beautiful,' she sighed, and stayed there, looking out. Albert was shown to his room.

Evening had brought drafts of cool air by the time they went down to dinner. Just two people awaited them in the big salon. Introductions. Nadine began.

'Here is Albert Exodus, my fiancé. Albert, Mr Meridian.'

The man before them loomed rather than stood. He wore gray velvet of a rather old-fashioned cut: wide lapels, matching gilet, a gold chain across the paunch. His head was conical, hairless and so large that it burdened even the broad neck and shoulders it rested on. He waved a ringed hand toward his companion.

'My friend Ritter,' was the way he introduced him. The other was clearly just that: my friend Ritter.

Conversational bits and pieces floated in the big room, still warm from the desert afternoon. Ritter didn't say much. He saw no reason to. He was one of those fortunate beings who exude confidence; in fact, he was up to his ears in love with himself. Dressing in the morning was a tender and absorbing event. Even the buttons on his shirt, lovingly fastened, seemed to be medals of excellence. His thin hair was nothing less than a halo, even if it was barely visible; and he almost felt sorry for the sprouting hairs that had to be shaved off his face. Was he not, he asked himself, simply a careful custodian of this superb physical envelope? So he blandly listened as Meridian outlined life at Windcote: there were two more occupants, Meridian's daughter, age seven, and her governess shared the top floor. He laughed. 'Governess is a big word for the person in question. But so she is called.' These comments seemed uttered for himself alone, and he quickly changed the subject. A dim mealtime followed. More guests would arrive in the morning. He outlined plans for riding, described his favorite trails.

'Of course anyone can go off on his own, you know, there's no limit to the desert,' and he added, glancing at Nadine, 'or its surprises.'

The evening wound down in desultory talk. Amber lamps lit small patches of the salon, a room so vast that it lost most of itself in shadowy nothingness. Nadine was half hidden in a chiaroscuro that breathed across the furniture,

Meridian the presence that talked and gestured for the girl beside him. Ritter was yawning. Albert rose unsteadily. His eyes sought the familiar face, saw it smile. Then:

'I'm staying a while, Albert. There's so much to learn before our ride tomorrow.'

He didn't see Nadine the next morning. She had already gone out by the time he went to her door. Other people came, bringing their voices, shards of music; even the slamming of doors had a congenial air. He had risen early after a night of unfinished dreams. Out in the corral he talked with José, the Mexican stableman who seemed glad to have a listener. His stories were fragmented and some-times lurid, a mixture of lore and hearsay, but he knew the neighboring canyon, its spirits and its contours, by heart. He rode until afternoon. Returning his horse to the stable, he asked, 'Have you seen the young miss?' José looked at him for a moment before answering. Then, turning away to attend to the horse, he muttered a simple 'No.' At tea time Albert knocked on her door and looked in. There was no one.

Evening was still a sunset away when Albert entered the dining room. Shadows were long. The table's crystal and silver held daylight's last prisms of color – a room that seemed to hold its breath before imminent occupation by its diners. Yet was so quiet. Albert's mind was filled with voices, the voice of Meridian the evening before, and Nadine's flat little trill to say she was 'staying a while'. What had happened to her? Why did she bring him to this outlandish place? Above all, how had she become so mesmerized by this hulk of flesh, this imitation of a man? He had decided to find out at once. He would put it to her, now: he would leave Windcote in the morning.

With an air of high resolve he stepped carefully, almost on tiptoe, the upper part of his body thrust forward, intent. So preoccupied, he didn't see the man still sitting by the window. Moving around the table he bent down at each place-setting to examine the card by the plate, his narrow face with its coquettish beard alert as a bird in high grasses. He stopped at the place he sought, on the right of Meridian's princely chair, and bringing from his pocket a folded paper, he slipped it under the napkin. As he drew back, his hand still on the table, his eyes, glancing up, met those of his host, and for an eternity he didn't move at all.

'Aren't you early for dinner, Exodus?' came the voice from its nest of drapery, continuing in a monotone, 'and full of romantic ideas, well, well. Not what I would have expected from a fellow like you. Kid stuff! Come, my young friend, let's see what sort of pabulum you've dreamed up. Maybe I can offer some useful suggestions. Do bring it here.'

Albert stood silent. 'Speak up, man,' went on the drawling voice. 'Maybe your passion has driven you to poetry. A charming last resort. But there are places ... I had better tell you ... poems don't ring true out here, no matter how shell-like the ear. The desert has, well, an effect on it. It burns for other sounds, sounds I doubt you know how to make. Or—'

'Who are you?' brought out Albert. 'What are you doing to Nadine?' He didn't recognize his own voice.

'What a funny question!' Meridian held his package tighter. 'But you seem a little hysterical, the desert sun, it—'

'Oh for God's sake leave the sun out of this. No, I'm not hysterical. I'm baffled and disgusted. Yes, and I'm driven to writing notes. Something's happened to Nadine. She came here to commune with nature. Yes, that's the way she saw it: nature. She has an obsession with it, some sort of longing ...'

'Then you should respect it.'

'It's just that: do you think I would have brought her here if I didn't? I respect it because it's unattainable; that is, in the way she sees it.'

Meridian half smiled. 'Nature is something she should be allowed to define for herself. Especially where to find it.'

Albert felt he was staring into an abyss of defeat, yet he went on, 'This house, sir, is utterly alien to anything natural, and I'm going to get her out of it!'

Meridian had risen and was now standing at the door, the tube-like package under his arm, his head a little to one side, musing.

'You have courage, I see, an admirable trait,' he said quietly. 'But I really must warn you: everything is different here. Everything.' He turned to go, then paused. 'By the way, I'll be grateful for a bit of, shall we say, conviviality tonight. Please remember that the guest owes a little something to the occasion. There's nothing more deadly that a gloomy dinner partner.'

He stood in the doorway, filling it, backlit from the hall beyond. 'Particularly here where my dinners are so carefully planned.' And though it was almost dark he added as he went, 'Good afternoon.'

Albert stayed – five minutes, fifteen? – staring down at the blur of crystal and silver and linen. An Indian housemaid in a sagging skirt and turquoise ornaments appeared carrying a bowl of yellow roses, set it on the table, and padded out. Yellow roses. He gazed at them as at some prodigy, some conjured weeds that would confess to being cacti. Still he didn't move. Sounds of laughter came from the terrace. He lifted his head, rubbed his beard for a moment, then drew the slip of paper from under the napkin and left the room.

Hurrying, he strode across the hall and through the cluttered salon, bumping into a shaky table, brushing an armchair, setting up a whining protest from the harp by the door. He looked at his watch. Half past seven. Still at least an hour before dinner. It occurred to him that he might not come down. Would it matter? An annoyance?

Or even a relief? But he knew even before he had time to play with the notion that he would come. He would sit in his appointed place, to watch and to wonder at his own forbearance.

A numbing disbelief invaded him as he observed himself moving through these rooms, a disbelief shaping itself into an abiding question: what am I doing here? But instead of an answer there was only a familiar opacity. Of old questions, like stone flags that hung in the air absurdly suspended, stones in levitation, of all shapes, weightless against the limpid backdrop of the void. It was his collection. He, Albert, collector of stone questions. Lying in their velvet depths, his perhaps precious stones?

What am I doing here? He saw his studio, his workplace. Because Albert was a painter. Like an amateur alchemist hidden away with his boiling chemicals, his sulfurs, their nauseous emanations, so, at times, Albert hid himself with his paints and mediums. He played at being the catalyst; he was intoxicated with the odors of turpentine, varnishes, oils, siccatives, alcohols. All the reality of these humble necessities of the painter's art intrigued him. He would spend long hours in his secret olfactory paradise. Secret and perverse, as no picture was ever painted there.

He would come into the room toward eleven in the morning, lock the door, and put on an apron. Then, at a table littered with bottles, cans, brushes, knives and tubes, he squeezed out the beautiful colors on a paper palette, always squeezing out too much, prolonging the voluptuous gesture. A long worm of barite green came with two soft plops on the palette. He mixed this with another snake of vermilion. These fused to produce something gray, a gray of mud and iron, stone gray, like the desert rocks of Ethiopia he remembered from some picture-book in which they writhed in all their cruel dimensions. He made hundreds of drawings, invisible on black paper, and piled them carefully behind the door, not before numbering them with black ink. During one entire winter he had painted with his left hand. There was no change, the frustration was exquisite. Another time he had spent the whole day painting his forearm cobalt blue. That evening it was bandaged as he sat at dinner. But these experiments produced nothing but further opacity, and no sign was offered to appease his demons.

Standing now at the foot of the wide staircase, his face lifted, listening to the voices that spun out their nearness in the warm air of the terrace, he heard Meridian's suave accents. As he started up the stairs the memory of several hours earlier came between him and the flight of steps: the figures of the little girl and her governess, walking up the same steps, sedate, withdrawn but sharing, he was certain, the tangle and tide of Windcote's days and nights. He knew then that he must see her, the governess, at once. The more he thought of her, of the stolid architecture of her face with its comatose eyes that looked past him, the more he felt that under that mask lay the answer he needed to cut, once and for all, the thread of his present concern. Through her he might learn what he now wanted to know, had to know. She would surely betray, by some sign or some word, her own involvement, and the key would drop like a leaf on his hand.

4

He moved now with purpose. Up the stairs and through the winding third-floor corridor. There were no lights – the corridor was dark as a cave. Under a door gleamed a yellow sliver of light. He knocked.

No one answered. For several minutes he stood in the shadows, feeling himself without substance, aware only of his thoughts pulsing against the dark. He knocked again, this time louder, and was surprised to feel his heart leap in his chest – it made him smile at himself. He lifted his hand to knock again but instead drew back, turned around, and began to walk away.

It was then that the door partly opened. A streaming radiance fell before him on the scrolled carpet. Someone said, 'Who is there?'

Albert turned suddenly shy, head bent, blinking in the light. Nelly stood in the doorway, her hand firmly on the knob. A flowered bandanna was tied around her head. 'Who is it?'

'It's me,' said the visitor. 'I mean my name is Albert. I've seen you on the stairs – you're the governess, aren't you?'

No answer from Nelly, who stood planted on her side of the door. Albert took a deep breath and began again: 'I'm sorry. I don't even know your name but ... I'd like to talk to you. It's important. I mean it's important to me ...'

Making an effort, Nelly brought her eyes to focus. She looked at Albert as if he were a picture to study at her leisure. Finally she spoke.

'It doesn't seem like you should be here at all. These are a little girl's rooms. Maybe you didn't know that,' whereupon she smiled and threw the door wide. 'But come in if you want to so much.'

He thanked her and stepped inside. Lights blazed everywhere. From at least a dozen wall sconces besides numerous lamps and a crystal-laden chandelier the light streamed, scalded the room as if to purify the outlandish furniture and bric-a-brac that exploded into every corner. Though a big room – the place might have been a kind of hall or even a ballroom – it was nearly overpowered by the mantelpiece that rose, like some separate architectural folly, to the domed ceiling. Without a single straight line, spurning any hint of symmetry, it occupied the wall with much the same sort of random form as a twist of smoke. In its design there was no reference to nature, no leaves, fruits, flowers, animals, birds, no volutes or familiar arabesques in its carving; just an unsettling hint of another world where birds and flowers, if not unknown, were surely unloved. On the hearth, where on winter nights a fire might burn, there was now what appeared to Albert a tangled heap of birds' wings, dusty and half-feathered.

Nelly continued gazing at him for a few minutes while he too had nothing to say. She cleared some garments from a gilt chair and motioned to him to sit down. Albert blinked in the harsh light, too dazed to make out the outlandish surroundings. An oriental carpet covered the floor. Hovering upon it in the wildest profusion was furniture of enough periods and provenance to give it an air of finicky collecting ... though the collector apparently disdained the last two centuries, there being only a few small bronzes from the classical revival, a black armoire (Spanish?) leaning crookedly by the far wall. Everywhere the eye met a vertiginous dazzle of gilt chairs, mirrors, a painted commode, terribly silent clocks of bronze and porcelain, a number of shapely tables. Upon all of these tables lay myriad smaller objects in wonderful disorder, and on the chairs as well, several of them lying on their backs, legs in the air serving as more racks for the apparently inexhaustible litter of rags, garments, shoes, boxes, jars, a birdcage, umbrellas, a Mexican saddle, several wigs, a tail of horsehair, chessmen, phonograph records, a pale brocade coat in tatters. Albert didn't see anything but blaze. If he saw the scene at all it was a kaleidoscopic flash that needed only a shake to turn into something else. This room and its burdens were no more than meaningless trash. If he had come here to gather knowledge it was not a mild quest. In that sense he was, as he would say later, a hunter, not a gatherer.

Gradually Albert brought his eyes to focus. There was a glass-enclosed bookcase to the left of his chair. But it held, he saw, only one of those dim sets of identically bound brown books, running from A to something, probably a once-complete encyclopedia. The rest of the case was crammed with rubbish. Through an open door far away to the left Albert glimpsed another room; it too was brightly lit. Probably the child's own room . . .

'I would let you play the phonograph,' said Nelly politely, 'but the little girl is having her dinner and she doesn't like music while she eats. It makes her sick. Besides, we've just had a row' – she nodded significantly toward the other room – 'and it takes a lot of patience to quiet her down. She's high strung.' Nelly looked at him in a way that suggested he was very much out of place.

'Perhaps I'd better go,' said Albert and half rose. 'I could come back later.'

'Oh, don't do that,' said Nelly, finally waking up. 'There's no harm in a quiet talk. I don't mind in the least. Besides, you won't always be at Windcote, and anyway I'm not sure I'll let you in again, so you may as well sit here a bit. D'you have a cigarette?'

Albert jumped up and began fumbling through his

pockets. 'I'm afraid—' he began, but she was already looking away.

'Never mind. And sit down.'

He murmured an apology, sat down, and said all at once in a resolute tone, 'How long have you been here?'

She was looking at him, eyes half closed, humming a little under her breath. 'I like your beard,' she said affably. 'It's distinguished.'

'Thank you.' Albert shifted in his chair then leaned forward again. 'But tell me, have you been here a long time?'

She gazed dully. 'Here?'

'Yes. Here at Windcote.' He felt as if he were trying to communicate through water.

'Oh, a pretty long time, I guess. That is, sometimes it seems like a long time. And then again—' She smiled.

Albert looked at her, astonished. 'But don't you know how long you've been living here – weeks, months, years? Surely you remember when you came ... '

'In the summer!' said Nelly, coming to the surface. 'They brought me in the Cadillac from the train. It was the hottest day I've ever seen. Really, scorching hot!' She shook her head, remembering that scorching hot day in the summer.

Albert stared. Then, suffused with something like embarrassment, he lowered his gaze. He saw himself and the situation as equally absurd, yet after a moment looked up at Nelly. Moving his chair closer to hers, 'Tell me,' he pronounced the words distinctly, 'do you have a calendar?'

'No, he won't have one in the house. He says they're useless here. He says they don't tell me anything.'

'Does *he* know when you came?'

'Oh, why be so pesky! Maybe he does. But I wouldn't ask him. Why should I? He hates questions like that. And he's been good to me, really good. Why, if it weren't for him I might still be in the home – I was in The Good Shepherd Home for Delinquent Girls, you know.' She said this as if mentioning a boarding school. 'Oh, but I'm not common. My father was a professor, they told me that at the home. "You must make your poor dead father proud of you," they said. So I was really good at my lessons. And when I left I was first in deportment and neatness.'

'Did he come and get you there?'

'Yes,' said Nelly, warming, 'I was fed up. Really fed up. I guess he saw that. He talked to me in the reception room. He said he would educate me and that I would be with his little girl. So I left that very day on the train. I'm an orphan,' she added proudly.

'Of course.' Albert fell silent, as though he were reading her words in a book. They were almost visible, the milky filaments of her mind, the unhurried flowing of her pink blood. It was all more than he had hoped for and still not enough; it was too much and yet opaque. Struggling with ragged clues, a dozen questions begged for utterance. Could he dare one more?

The girl was growing restless. She began to hum again,

48

suddenly stood up, and moved around behind his chair. She leaned down, her breast pressing against his shoulder, and spoke into his ear.

'How about us playing the phonograph now?'

Albert jumped up from the chair and spun around facing her. 'But you said you couldn't, it's not allowed. Don't you remember?'

'I've got a swell record. Just drums. We could dance.'

Dry and suffocating as it was, her lymphatic approach did not deter him. Straining for nonchalance, he brought himself to smile. He even put out a hand to grasp hers.

'Please sit down for just another minute,' he begged. She looked cross. He pulled at her hand. 'Come on. We can finish our chat first . . . '

'It's finished,' said Nelly, very much withdrawn.

He tried again. 'There's something I can tell you,' he said archly. 'Something nice—' not wanting to see that he had clearly slipped out of her confidence.

'Not interested,' frowned Nelly.

There was no hope for it, the girl wasn't going to talk. So, risking nothing, he threw out another question.

'Look. You're a very smart girl, anyone can see that. In fact, why, you know, I would have guessed right away you were the daughter of, well, at least a professor. But just tell me now, about Meridian, does he really educate you? Do you have daily lessons? Or evening ones, maybe? I mean, for instance, what do you study?'

At this a thin hard glaze poured over the features of Nelly's face and it became a perfect mask. The change was so abrupt and so complete that even the texture of her skin took on a waxy glacial look. She folded her arms across her bosom and simply stared past him. Finally she smiled, remotely, slightly one-sided, and said, 'Why do you ask me that? What are you getting at, anyway?'

'Oh, I thought if—'

'Don't bother. It's time for you to go now or you'll be late for dinner. And that won't do at all. Bye bye now.' She patted him on the shoulder while pushing him to the door. In the same moment a small voice called out behind them.

'Who is that?'

Albert turned. In the doorway at the far end of the room stood a white figure, the little girl, sharply focused in the bright light. Her pretty head was lifted, her pose imperious. She held a fork in her right hand. The two by the door looked at her in silence, baffled, as if caught out in some prank. Nelly spoke. 'A visitor. Just someone come to pay us a teeny little visit—'

'Be quiet!' broke in the little girl. She advanced toward them, looking steadily at Albert. 'I was asking you. What's your name?'

'Albert. Albert Exodus. I came to call on your governess and I'm just leaving.'

'Well, you better stay.'

'I'm so sorry,' he smiled. 'But I really can't. You see, I have to—'

'You stay!' insisted the child. 'You can come in my room with me.' He felt his arm pressed from behind and turned to Nelly, who looked nervous. She whispered, 'Go on. Go on in with her.'

Albert, amazed by it all, didn't see any reason to stay longer. It was late already and he had to freshen up for dinner. How many hours, days even, had he been trapped in this stifling cage? His thoughts needed sorting out; another part of them was already downstairs, involved in a different drama. He felt no wish to stay here prattling with a child, but now there was a dismal urgency in Nelly's erstwhile expressionless face; she looked frightened. He saw there a way to restore himself to her favor. And to come back ...

'Oh very well, then. Just for a few minutes.' Shrugging and resigned, he followed the child as she picked her way through the clutter and came to the room beyond.

If he had expected a different ambiance here he was soon disabused of that notion, for the scene before him exactly matched the one he had just left, with, if possible, an even heavier load of dejected paraphernalia: the same gilt chairs, cumbrous hangings, expired clocks, the same jungle of shaky tables with just one point in common – their uselessness. There was nowhere anything to suggest that this was the home of a child: no dolls, no toys, no diminutive furniture of the sort that generally delights the heart of a little girl. Oddly, there was no carpet either, so that, hesitating in embarrassed chaos on the bare floor, everything had an even sorrier look of impermanence and waiting.

In a semicircular alcove of leaded windows, a small table, lace covered, was laid out for dinner: a plateful of food, untouched, a napkin, a tiny glass of red wine. Here he was invited to sit down.

He moved toward the window seat, but the little girl stopped him, pointing to her own chair, saying in the gentlest possible voice, 'No, you sit here. You're going to eat my dinner.'

Albert couldn't help laughing. 'What an idea! So I'm going to eat your dinner. Well, I thank you, that's very kind, but I'm afraid I can't accept. You see, I have a dinner of my own to eat, downstairs.'

He began to feel really annoyed as the child stared her displeasure. Of course it wasn't serious, but the suggestion, or rather demand, unnerved him.

'Yes, you have to eat it. And while you're doing that I'll show you my memory box.'

'I'll be very glad to see your memory box,' said Albert. 'Do bring it here.'

'I can't,' said the girl sadly. 'Not unless you eat.'

'But my dear child,' he pronounced his words slowly, 'I am not going to eat your dinner.'

52

He asked himself why he had come in, just to be harangued by this odd child with her satin shoes and feverish eyes. They were all he saw, those eyes. He wondered how it could be that he, Albert, looked into them with such confusion, twin lamps in a dark nowhere, disembodied and unbearable – yes, unbearable – and their possessor behind them, coming near him now. She put her hand on his, reminding him.

'If you don't do as I want I'll tell Papa.' She gazed solemnly at the astonished Albert. 'I mean it. I'll tell Papa you came here and he'll be mad.'

Albert stood up. He looked around for Nelly, yes, even Nelly, for his sense of the moment and the event was all at once unreliable. He faced the girl.

'Do you realize this is blackmail? Do you know what that is?'

'I don't care. I don't care what it is. I just want you to eat for me.' Looking down at the floor, she added, 'Papa doesn't like you anyway, and he'd have a fit if I told him you'd been up here.'

'Why do you say that? How do you know your papa doesn't like me?' he asked in amazement.

'Because,' she tossed her hair, 'because he doesn't like any of the men that come out here. He despises them. He says they're *inferior*.'

The last word was pronounced 'unfairier', and Albert quite realized she didn't know its meaning, but the words filled his head with new thoughts. Again he seemed close to the answers he had come for. Weary, and with a sudden headache, he asked, 'Now what is it you want me to do?'

How the child brightened! The troubled frown left her face and she gave him a smile of such stunning grace that he trembled, and was surprised at the trembling, and at what was happening to him.

'Don't you remember, you silly man?' she said gently. 'Just sit down here and eat this dinner.'

Dumbfounded, he watched himself, as it were, walk back to the table, sit down, and swallow a forkful of meat. He gazed at the little glass of wine, then picked it up and drained it at a gulp. He had forgotten that the entire performance was a mockery and a bribe as he sat there swallowing the food like a starving beggar, his eyes unseeing, and his head bowed over the plate. Not until every morsel had disappeared did he lay down the knife and fork. Even after the girl had come close, holding a cherub-painted tin box, he still did not look up but sat motionless, staring at the empty plate.

'Don't you want to see my memory box?' she whispered.

He turned away from the table and looked at her face. His gaze lost itself in the eyes, the throat, the hair, the white dress, as he devoured the plateful of food. She waited there without surprise, always smiling.

'Come over here,' putting her arm across his shoulder, 'let's go sit on the sofa. I'll show you the things in the box.'

And he allowed himself to be led away once more. Trancelike, his spirit possessed by an overwhelming torpor, he did her bidding like a dog. Sitting beside her, the perfume of her presence enveloping him in a haze, he watched her open the box while her words as she prattled came to his ears as unearthly music. That the objects were of a surpassing strangeness affected him not at all. While she reached into the box, pulling out bits of fur, the claws and tails of gila monsters, skins of reptiles, spotted eggs, even single eyes preserved in tiny jars, nothing reached him but the eerie silver web of her voice and the superb reality of her nearness.

'Here is a lovely one, it belonged to a coyote. Anyway, I think it's lovely.' She held out one of the jars.

'Yes,' said Albert, 'I think so too.'

The eye floated in a creamy gelatinous fluid. As she put it away she said to him, 'I'm glad you like them. I knew you would. No one – really no one – but you has ever seen them, specially not Nelly. Oh, she wants to! It makes her sick that I have secrets. I know she sneaks in here and hunts for my box. But let her! She'll never find it. You won't tell her about it, of course I know you won't.' She wrapped him again in her dazzling smile. 'Now I'm going to show you the best of all. My friend brought it just today.'

Running over to a painted credenza that held a stuffed owl she reached under a wing and took out a small something wrapped in blue paper.

'Nelly tried to take it away from me this afternoon. I was in the dining room downstairs. My friend had just brought it to me outside.'

Very daintily she opened the paper to show him another eye: the honey-colored iris, the pupil contracted almost to vanishing, the blue-white globe, veined with red and sticking to the paper. She began pulling away the stained paper fragments.

'What sort of creature did it come from?'

'Oh, I don't know that ... but do you like it?'

'Of course I do,' looking into her wonderful eyes. 'It's easily the best so far ...'

The littered room rocked before his vision; outlines waved, merged and dissolved while only the figure of the girl, fixed and tangible, was there beside him. Close yet remote as a nova she sat in her redolent aura while he was saying 'so far'. Yes, so far, because he too would be a 'friend', speak her language, share her secrets. He too would bring her a present to wrap in blue paper, another talisman to fill a little jar.

Taking her hand, 'Your treasures are wonderful, but I can bring you a better one still. I'm your friend too ...'

For a moment she was silent. She looked down at the box, laid the great yellow eye inside and closed the lid. Then she turned her face up to his.

'Yes, you're my friend now. My private friend. Otherwise I wouldn't show you *these*. But my other friend is different.

He's the only one who can bring me things. You couldn't do that. You couldn't.'

'But why, tell me why? Do you think I haven't the courage? Or the—'

He checked himself – he had almost said 'the love'.

'It isn't that,' she whispered. 'You couldn't be like my other friend because he's an animal.'

Albert stared. 'An animal?'

'Oh, now you know everything! Now I really better trust you. If you ever tell Nelly!' She was pleading with him. 'But you wouldn't! Please say you won't tell.' There were actual tears in her eyes.

'No,' Albert murmured, 'I won't tell anybody.'

He didn't want to look at her tears. Bending over, he put his face in his hands and sat folded on the sofa.

'Please sit up,' said the child, kneeling before him. Finding a remnant of his voice he told her to dry her tears. This she did while he straightened and she patted the cushions, going on about the friend that was an animal, a yellow sort of cat, kind and gentle and bigger than herself. 'He lives in the canyon and I ride over to see him there sometimes. When I can't go – I have to get away from Nelly – why then he comes here. I talk to him, I tell him everything, and he understands. And then he brings me these things. He never comes without bringing me something. Oh, he's a good friend. But not like you . . . ' She looked up at Albert with a tranquil gaze and took his thin hand in her two small ones.

Slowly he felt his calm returning and, with it, a sudden clarity of mind. He remembered, as one awakening, his identity, how he had come here, the dinner party downstairs.

'I have to leave now.'

She released his hand. 'Yes, I know. You have to go down and be with them. But you can come back—'

'Tonight,' he said, suddenly eager. 'I'll bring you a present . . .'

'Oh, no, not tonight . . .'

'But – tomorrow then.'

They walked together across the room. She opened the door and turned to him with grave ceremony. 'Goodbye, Albert. My name is Destina Meridian.'

He looked at her, fixing her face in his mind, 'Goodnight, Destina.'

There was no sign of Nelly in the outer room as he stepped over the carpet and closed the door behind him.

Coming down to the second-floor landing he heard two voices raised in what seemed surely a dispute immediately changed to banter upon his approach. Albert's ears registered the tone just as his eyes saw the doors, the carpet, the wainscoted walls, the two people watching him. They moved away from each other, addressing him with that conviviality so dear to habitual partygoers.

'Greetings!' boomed the man. 'You're probably looking for your door – can we help? I'm Ralph Vine and this is Maya.'

Closer now, he saw them: the man Vine, mustached, ruddy, eyes deeply planted under the bushes of his brow, the woman fleshy-fragile, round-eyed, and clearly held together by clever straps, pins, elastic and what must have been iron will. Of course Albert had heard of Ralph Vine. Although a face like Vine's would normally have little chance of attracting anyone, his, even for someone who didn't read the papers, had somehow groped its way into the public mind's eye like blindness. Pancaked to a warm bronze and capped by a generous wig that didn't quite match his own hair peeping from underneath, the face was a logo, advertising itself. He had been bagged for this remote weekend by Maya (the only name she owned to), an actress on the wane who had staked him in some former squeeze, amounting to a rescue. It was even rumored back in the city that they shared some activity having nothing to do with either public relations or the theater. Meridian had arranged their visit, with private plane and limousine. Ritter would be there. There were urgent matters, decisions to be made.

As they stood there in his path, Albert replied calmly. Clearer now, the corridor, the two people, the hour, had all become real to him; he talked and listened, especially listened as more strands of Windcote's web were cast around him in this second-floor hallway full of closed doors. Ralph Vine. Of course. One knew of him. Knew that if he had not invented public relations he had certainly brought them to a summit of power and even glory. He was jokingly referred to as corporate's first-aid for the way he could save a tottering career or wangle a client into Korea's trade program or Iran's ambassadorial community.

A few more idle remarks filled the necessary little void that preceded their parting, words about meeting for dinner.

5

Evening had finally dropped on Windcote like a drawn blind. Lamps were on in the long reception room and the terrace wall of glass gave back nothing but self-conscious reflections of people straggling in, shyly for the most part, feeling theatrical, not quite themselves. The women eyed each other, trying to remember who was who and which ones to make up to. One or two, especially, needed all the aplomb they could muster to carry off what was supposed to be their off-hand disguises – disguises that, in fact, disguised nothing and no one. For one, Maya was still anyone's dyed and trussed and painted Maya in her voluminous cloud of netting – sewn with feathers, butterflies and beetles – that she fussily believed reflected the present ambiance.

Nadine, on the arm of Meridian, sparked a mild gasp for the tangle of brown rags draping her body, a kind of burlap, torn to show windows to herself: a pale shoulder, a nipple, a navel.

For a contrast of a truly surprising nature, an unadorned

woman – Meridian called her simply 'the baroness' – sat alone by the piano as if she had been left there long ago like a piece of undusted furniture, ignored and ignoring, her face weathered to the hue of bronze leather with a fine network of wrinkles. Old? But how old? Her very simplicity was a disguise in this odd company where the others were making such efforts to distinguish themselves – a somber embarrassment, in faded black, with a little veiled hat trembling on her short gray hair like a fallen bird's nest of twigs.

At first, Ritter went to her grandly, said something that she seemed not to hear, though she smiled. Of course, he mused walking away, hard of hearing at her age, as he turned to Maya who was grateful for notice by that time.

A recent arrival was Chichi Palmer. This Chichi, (Sheshe, Cheeky, Chicky) was in need of money. Though her outlandish fees from modeling had carried her along so far, it wasn't nearly enough to support Chichi, whose habits and lifestyle were ever more expensive and demanding. Some help was needed just to keep her going, and going. She had heard about other ways to important income, ways that involve some very cunning secrets; but these, she had been assured, she needn't bother her pretty head about. Did she know Ralph Vine? Ralph Vine would fill her in, and he was to be at Windcote. So if she too were at Windcote, something would have to happen.

A phone call, a flight on Saturday morning – even

earlier, alas, than her work calls – and an hour-long, hideously bumpy ride in the Land Rover brought her, surprised and uneasy at being so far away from concrete and flash bulbs, to her dubious destination. There she was, in her tan satin skin and her big black gaze, unconcerned with disguises, and justifiably so, for at this moment she needed nothing but the diamond embedded in her chalky front tooth to denote her authority in matters of appearance.

Albert had not come in, to Meridian's annoyance; so with a murmured remark in Nadine's ear he led the way to the dining room. Seated, he surveyed the brilliance of his table and found it splendid. Nadine's presence at his right tightened the muscles in his throat and spun him around in her glow like a twig in a whirlpool. For him, she marked this table and this evening with an unbearable promise. As the collector of rare moths thrills at his find of the rarest of specimens, so was Meridian possessed by anticipation of the pinning.

Did he not already possess her hair, first step in his direction, his obsession? He had felt it from the moment he saw her, that hair. It would have to be his. It would begin with his ritual of cutting.

After their morning ride, when heat and his strange words had made her drowsy and confused, Nadine went to the pool. She was about to plunge when he loomed before her brandishing a scissors.

'Not yet,' he brought out, 'it mustn't get wet.'

She laughed a little. 'What mustn't get wet?'

'The hair. Not before it's to be cut.'

This time she didn't laugh. 'What do you mean? Who said anything about my hair, or cutting it, of all things . . . ?'

She sat down on a patio chair, he followed and talked to her again in those unfamiliar phrases: about hair, its magic, its power. Nadine frowned.

'I'd call that a hair fetish,' she said matter-of-factly.

'Call it what you will. But I am asking you now: let me cut your hair.'

'Why?'

'Because I want it. I want it more that anything in this world.'

Why anyone would say such a thing was too weird for Nadine even to consider. But she had often thought, like any girl, of cutting her hair. One doesn't risk anything: hair grows back. After all, why not, if it was that important to someone – a rather special someone, at that? So while the sun poured its rays over Windcote, Nadine's long pale hair poured into the hands of Raoul Meridian as he wielded the shaking scissors. That all this had happened only hours before, afternoon being given over to siesta, was reason enough to shock Albert, who had finally arrived, into disbelief. Here she was, laughing, talking and bearing her foolish garb with the good-natured spirit of teamwork in a game; prelude to his master plan, thought Meridian,

64

who wanted for nothing at this moment. His business with Ritter and Ralph Vine would not take long; some addresses to exchange, names, a few directives. A long night was before him.

On his left Chichi gazed across the table at Vine the way one looks at the approaching taxi in the rain. She was sure that he would take her on. Plans need people like Chichi, she told herself, moving her finger around the rim of her wine glass, drawing out that sweet thin sound like a faraway bell. Her thoughts were soon interrupted by a voice speaking to her: Ritter, at her left, a cologne-drenched reminder of familiar places, a touchstone of appointments, flight schedules, codes and stratagems, his flashing glasses and impeccable business suit sending out a dull message as he turned to her, saying with hearty assurance:

'Ritter.' He thrust out his hand which Chichi looked at wonderingly. 'Ritter the robot, Ritter the chameleon. Ritter, your friend from now on.'

No one appeared to notice Albert when he entered the room and slipped into his place. Wine glasses were clinking along with talk and laughter. Two women in black home-spun and bare feet were about to remove the bisque. Albert nodded an apology to his neighbors and seized a spoon, dipping it into the pink soup. But as he raised it to his lips he frowned and laid the spoon down, gazing at nothing as the dish was carried away. He leaned back, grateful to be unnoticed, and reached out to his glass of pale wine, twirling it on the cloth, whereupon a clear, familiar drawl cut in from the head of the table.

'Exactly, dear girl! It's the same mawkish style among some of our young fellows. They seem to think ignoring the amenities could attract some special attention. Is it to distinguish themselves, impress someone, maybe? I can't imagine what they're after. So impetuous! They sulk, they fling innuendoes like naughty schoolboys with paper wads, they appear at any old time for dinner ... Ah, now I have it – color! It lends them color. Or is it substance?' He leaned forward, meekly inquiring. 'Come, Exodus, we're curious – what's the reward? You're the specialist in these mysteries.'

'I didn't think I was a specialist in anything.'

Meridian seemed not to hear. 'After all,' he insisted, 'we might be wrong. It may be something ... different?'

'Why yes,' Albert raised his voice. 'It's certainly different. But how can I tell you? You live in the desert. For this you'd have to know something of the jungle.'

'Oh, I've been in the jungle,' cried Maya. 'We were touring the—'

'Fascinating,' went on Meridian, ignoring the interruption. 'Torridly fascinating. And have you just come in from that jungle? Is that what kept you so long? Tell us what kept you.'

All were looking now at Albert, idly curious like children watching a party magician. 'Tell us,' repeated Meridian slowly, 'where have you been so long?'

The two might have been alone at the table. Albert did not see the other faces but looked directly into the eyes of his host.

'I've been playing with a lion.'

No one spoke. Maya laughed a little, then whispered something to Ritter beside her. This made him exchange a knowing wink with Vine across the table. The mood was playful, of course. Everyone knew it was all a game. Albert missed nothing of this and, as from a distance, was amazed at his own indifference – to Nadine, especially. That the person in burlap rags was the same girl he had brought here only yesterday, the Nadine who had caused him such anguish hardly three hours before, she who had been the object of his tenderness for many months and was now only a foggy illusion that his memory would not accept; all this was sadly true.

'You don't seem the lion type,' called out Chichi from down the table, and to Albert's puzzled glance she repeated rather impatiently, 'I said you aren't the lion type. I wouldn't have guessed you as having a cat affinity at all. More like a caribou or a deer. The milder sort. Something vulnerable but fast. . . . ' She tilted her head back and smiled broadly. The diamond sparkled.

'The young man is right,' came from the baroness, suddenly waking up. She set down her glass with precision. 'Believe him! Do you think the jungle's a word, a drum on the other side of the world? No, no, no!' pointing at the long windows behind her. 'The jungle is out there too, under the desert's memory. I know a few things, and who else here could remember anyway?'

The talk had gradually taken on a focused bead, a target. Was this baroness whom nobody knew a piece of Meridian's theatrics, an entertainment, sitting there almost quaking with fervor? 'If you doubt me ask the stones and the sand, they'll tell you about the jungle. And for that matter, the forest too, and the waters ...'

'Yes, they're delusions, simply delusions,' put in Ritter, Ritter the robot, the chameleon. 'Have you ever driven through these areas, hoping for something to look at, *any-thing* ... and all you've seen are the signs: National Forest? Not a tree in sight. Not a shrub, not even a tumbleweed. Miles and miles of it, bald as the moon, but it pleases the nation to call it a forest. And by God, out there in the heat and the shimmer you begin to believe it—'

'That's not what I mean,' cried the baroness.

Ritter was carried away – 'And you've been in it all day and still those devilish signs, this is the forest, and you begin to see big trees, you hear monkeys screaming, and you brake the car just in time, when a lion slips from the mangroves to cross the road while a water snake falls in your lap ...' He was almost out of breath with admiration for his voice.

'You've quite an imagination!' Maya marveled. Her amazement seemed fittingly tangential to his own.

'Or a good memory,' put in Ralph Vine. 'In any case, with a little try you can see anything around here.'

Ritter preferred not to hear while basking in Maya's admiration. It made him feel appreciated. All too often he had been told that people like himself, immersed in the abstractions of business (shady or otherwise) and money (blessedly unqualified), had no imagination. So he had devoted some practice and thought to inventing one of his own. 'Oh well,' he threw this out like a philosophical bouquet, 'I guess these things happen to everyone. The power of suggestion, the runaway mind . . . '

'Not to me,' countered Maya, her feathers quivering with import. 'I always have to cultivate my hallucinations. If I'm in the desert – here, anyway – I don't see anything but sand. Aren't deserts supposed to have sheiks in them? In fact, I'm always looking for Rudolph Valentino. It seems so appropriate. But I never see him.' She looked sad.

'Let me suggest, my dear Maya,' said Meridian dryly, 'that you look for Valentino in Hollywood. He's probably in some moldy theater signing his photograph.'

'He's dead,' corrected Vine.

'True!' said Meridian, slouching. 'Does that make any difference, my dear?'

She lowered her eyes, embarrassed that he scorned her so publicly, never even asking herself if it was quite right of him to do so. In fact, there was something bluntly unquestioning about the general trend among

Meridian's acquaintances to accept him as monarch, not exactly saying 'he can do no wrong', but not allowing the thought even to be formed, much less the words to be uttered.

Maya was no exception in this, particularly now, when, wistful about her vanished youth, she must look elsewhere for compensation. And what other solace is there but money? For money she will swallow her pride and forget that once, on the occasion of her introduction to the laboratory, he had wrung from her the confession that to have an orgasm she needed to think about being in the deserted lounge of a film theater with one of those men who go to the movies alone. That they would lie on the musty divans of the lobby, locked in until morning, again and again in the big silent theater, only their own sounds breaking on the stale air. For Meridian it had been a blow to his sense of artistry not male pride. Of which he had none, believing the concept to be not only baseless but foolish. His erotic experiments with willing partners were, he thought, inspired, even ecstatic; once familiar with his laboratory, they could never again be seduced by simple flesh, no matter how inflamed. Maya had disappointed him. But she was an actress after all and, he reminded himself, had plunged with a good will into his very special games, though rather in the spirit of one tackling a new and difficult role.

But that was – when? This was now. His gaze came

back to Nadine. An unfamiliar weakness gained him for a moment, draining away his sense of himself. A stab of anticipation held him as he listened to her chatter. The baroness was still murmuring her outlandish incantations about snakes and lions, while Nadine, hands clasped under her chin, marveled.

'Fantastic!' she cried, and bent her head to the old woman as to a baby in its crib. 'How absolutely fantastic! Lions here. Why that's perfect. I suppose if I stay long enough I'll be seeing them too.' She turned to Meridian, 'Did you know that? There *are* lions in this desert. She has seen them!'

'Yes, and other things too,' the baroness muttered. She was staring at nothing. 'The desert is full to bursting. The sand talks to you but its words don't rhyme, the stones shed water and, I promise you, the commonest glass turns to amethyst. So tell me, what is the past? I'll tell *you*. It's a tide of ice that came and went, and little toads that still live buried in deathless breathing. They wait, yes, and their memories keep roaring of light and liquid air.' She looked around. 'You can smile, go on, smile! But men forget their names in the crevices of desert wind; they crumple like burning paper with frozen throats and eyes that roll in the sun. Their bones turn to chalk but they still come to lie down and feel hot breath on their faces and stars fall on their mouths.'

Ritter turned to murmur in Chichi's ear, 'A nice image

that, "stars falling on their mouths".' She glanced at him with weary disdain. The baroness went on in a low, dreamy tone:

'Stub your toe on a stumbling stone and cry. There's no harm done. Shake the sand from your hair and pick the cactus spine from your shirt. Laugh and say it isn't true. But in the red rock chasm you'll not have time to cry out. Your words will be heard only in the world you are coming to, wrapped in the dust of this one. I'm old and dry as dust myself. But I have seen big birds circling and I know they have a mathematics of their own. And I've seen lions walking on their four feet. I've seen Hopis flinging their snakes to the four winds. I've seen them and I grieved because they hid their secrets from me.'

She looked up, then turned her eyes on Nadine. 'They say I look with second sight. I have never been sure . . .'

Meridian had gone rather pale and laid down his knife and fork. 'The baroness is of the old school, language and all,' he hurried to inform them. And then, with an effort at ease, 'To be sure, there are still certain wild species around – of no great interest, really.'

'Small mountain lions, lynx, bobcats,' suggested Ritter. 'All rather nothing as lions go.'

'There you have it! Mere cats compared to the African species. Besides, even the mountain lion, the puma, is hardly ever seen anymore in these parts.'

'Oh but I have seen them and their yellow eyes,'

muttered the baroness, 'but it may have been a long time ago. I've never worn the skins of animals ... '

This last seemed to awaken Chichi. She looked for the first time at the baroness. Who was the old lady talking to? What was this buzzing old voice up to? 'What is she saying? What is all this?'

'Don't look at me,' said Ritter with some petulance.

'But what's it about, anyway?' She looked over at Vine. 'What's your take on this weird conversation?'

He frowned. 'I wouldn't call it a conversation, exactly.'

'It's nothing, my dear,' Meridian called out. 'The baroness is fond of metaphor, she likes to embroider the simplest fancy. Pay no attention.' He frowned, visibly flustered and not too satisfied with his own words; less than satisfied, too, with the presence of this odious old woman that he had himself invited and could not now chase away. He had to remember that as a 'family member' she was part of the bargain, that is, his signing on to keep her on the property in exchange for its fifty thousand acres. They would all be his when she died. It had been easy enough, though sometimes decidedly trying.

'Who is she, anyway?' Nadine suddenly asked. 'She reminds me of my Attacapa nanny—' She would have gone on had not Albert's voice cut in:

'I believe the mountain lion is still seen here.'

A silence dropped once again over the table, this time like a veil. A thin veil, to be sure, but curiously clinging, an immense sticky web that managed to stifle the air of the room. It was suddenly so warm. Maya fluttered her peacock fan. Ritter wiped his forehead. The old baroness was seized with coughing.

Everyone turned to Albert, whose words seemed to claw the tablecloth. Though his face was composed, a flush rose from his collar and stained the skin that covered his angular jaw. He had acquired at that moment what he had never wanted: the undivided attention of a number of people. But it didn't matter. How could it? He was far away from this dinner table, impelled by some obscure mechanism, his mind had leapt into a profile of the most staggering intention. He heard his own voice without knowing why he was talking. He saw the faces, monstrous now, all turned to him, pushing him to transform this insignificant evening into something with form and force. No matter if the form was born deformed. No matter if the force meandered – it would gather, it would not disappoint.

Meridian glared. 'Good heavens! Lions! Might I ask who has been deluding this fevered brain?' He waved his fat hand in Albert's direction, his elegant monotone masking exasperation – it was Albert, after all, who had brought him Nadine. Nadine . . .

'Three days ago a two-hundred-pound puma was shot, just sixty miles from here, near the Bar T Ranch. They found forty-two pounds of young beef in her stomach. I read it in a newspaper I found in the stable.'

'Oh, I'd love to see a lion!' Nadine broke in. 'A lonely yellow lion walking in the sand! I'm sure it would be poetical. A poetical image!' She actually looked down the table toward Albert.

Meridian pressed her arm. 'Don't forget, darling girl, one of the definitions of poetical is fanciful. This is utter nonsense,' he went on, 'some bored reporter's fun with words. My dear, there are no lions here. If there were I would give you one with a golden collar to lead it by – even a lion would lie down before you!'

'Like Una!' cried Maya. 'My first leading role. I played it at school. "Una and the Lion." I was thirteen. I remember, there were two boys inside the lion skin who wouldn't come out when the play was over. They took to going about in it. Wasn't that odd?'

'Oh la la! That wasn't odd, my dear lady, that was even!' snorted Ritter, and slapped his thigh with delight.

Albert had caught Meridian's words: there are no lions here. Lions are cats. A big cat can bring presents to a little girl. He frowned and stroked his forehead. The rooms on the third floor drifted again before his vision, the chaotic furniture, the diabolical mantelpiece, Destina's room, its light streaming in his brain. Again she sat close to him, her voice, her words, her child hands depriving him of breath. Again he felt her portent and was aghast. The havoc of her eyes as she said: 'he lives in the cliffs above the canyon.' The canyon ... the rose-red canyon ... and Albert knew all at once the fever of recognition. Those cliffs to the east of Windcote, the only sharp disturbance on the heaving sand, a wild rearing of jagged fantasy, crimson deep, mystery locked. He had come near its cleft that same morning when he had ridden the trail through the dry wash that abruptly ended at its throat ... 'and I go to see him there.'

A prodigious thought outlined itself in his mind. He looked up and smiled at Chichi. 'You're not the cat type,' she had said. Now, talking to Ritter, she felt Albert's careless gaze and returned it uneasily. There was an air of fever about him that was hard to reconcile with his earlier apathy. His stare was insolent. He began to laugh, soundlessly, his shoulders shaking. 'You're right, I'm not a cat,' he said to her, adding in a tone of irony, 'I'm a hunter,' and before the girl could answer Meridian had given the sign, dinner was over. Chairs were being pushed back and they were all leaving the table.

Albert was about to excuse himself when his host waved him away, 'Go on in with the ladies, Exodus, we have some dull matters to discuss.' Vine and Ritter, already serious, were busy lighting cigars. Albert bowed and left.

'In with the ladies,' was out on the terrace, where they had trailed one after the other, each one lugging her own preoccupations like tote bags in a late round of shopping, indifferent, with the barest attention to polite exchange. The night air and sleepy piping of the birds in the aviary jutting from the house made them languid and uncommunicative. In an angle of the shadowed wall someone strummed a guitar, hesitant, as if for himself, and his nasally, small voice whispered the words:

Por una ingrata, por una ingrata
Que me hay jugado una cruel traicion. . . .

The baroness, folded in on her prophecies and dreams, appeared to be sleeping. Chichi, pacing the length of smooth flagstone that might have been a fashion runway, held her shawl close and her impatience loosely. She waited only for the men, meaning Ralph Vine, to appear, rehearsing to herself the conversation they would have, had to have. Chichi would fill a role, she would make contacts, make certain that Vine would not be, well, fingered. And there was only tonight to decide it, because in the morning she would be on a plane.

Chichi need not have fretted: Vine would be on the same plane, as would the others – Maya and Ritter – on the New York plane, where there would be time and more time for the business of arrangement, whatever arrangement was yet to be made. All leave-taking would be done before parting for the night. The car was ordered for early morning and the four passengers would vanish from Windcote by sunup.

Maya, in fact, leaning against the parapet, watched the pacing girl with something more than casual curiosity.

Having put away the role of innocent wit (until the next dinner party) and laid down a magazine after idly flipping the pages back to front, she now felt a kind of woe, almost a premonition, while sizing up the striding figure before her. Ralph had mentioned her, 'a young person'.

Well, yes, she could be useful, she supposed. 'If you really think so,' she had said to him. It was hard to accept. After all, it was Maya herself who had always played the part of allurement, and now even Meridian was writing her off as useless. Why had she bothered with these itchy feathers and tulles? They didn't belong here under this overwhelming sky – nor did she. It was long since she had felt any charm in Windcote. The morning plane for New York would leave none too soon.

'Please come and sit down,' she said to Chichi.

Another figure stood far out in the shadows, making coaxing sounds to the birds in their big cage. Albert, coming out from the light, walked the length of the terrace and came close to her. He thrust his face down to her ear.

'You wanted to see a lion. I came to tell you I can show you one. Tonight if you like.'

As if her coaxing had drawn the words from a feathered throat inside the fragile prison, Nadine continued to tap and murmur to the birds. She did not turn to him but answered into the cage.

'How can I be sure? After all, it's not that easy to happen

on a wild animal, wherever it is. Besides, I'm told – you heard it yourself – they don't even exist here any more.'

Albert drew back. 'You've been told. I won't comment on what you've been told.' He looked at her now with weariness. 'But that's beside the point. I've made the offer. If you have other plans say so now, or if the idea frightens you then of course it's out of the question. But if you really want to see a lion I can show you one.'

She turned then and looked into his face. 'Are you so certain as all that?'

Albert's answer was steady. 'Why else would I propose it? Certainly not for myself. My feelings are elsewhere.'

Their eyes met in a deep merging exchange and Nadine said presently, 'Yes. You know I'm afraid of nothing. Anyway, what's there to be afraid of?' And she added after a pause, 'I'll go. But when? Now? Tonight?'

'Tonight. Come down to the little gulch just below the corral at, say, a quarter to one. The horses will be saddled and ready. Wear strong boots – we'll have to do some climbing.'

'Climbing? Not much, I hope. Shall I bring a gun?'

'No, I'll attend to that. I suppose I needn't ask you to say nothing of this to anyone.'

'Don't worry your head about that,' said the girl.

Albert turned and went in. For a few minutes she stood there still, tapping on the bars, whispering to the drowsy birds. A trill of laughter drifted out across the terrace, was picked up and tossed by a sudden warm wind. In the same moment, from somewhere came an urgent voice calling her name. *Nadine*! She turned and walked back toward the light, her shadow lengthening on the tiles.

From the guitar's broken heart love and lament followed on the night air:

> *Yo sin ti la muerte de seare*
> *y siempre en tus caricias*
> *pensando morire . . .*

6

What is a friend for Destina? She knows only that enemies are those who have stopped being children. She knows that because of them, moving in, right and righteous, demanding, clamoring for attention – because of these she must allow herself to be readied for bed by Nelly's indifferent ministrations, while her seven-year-old mind plays with seven-year-old thoughts that are at the same time ageless. They – the others – tell her she is seven years old. If every year she must remember to say a different number about herself, it is an order, something to obey, to say, to wear like a mask, keeping her own truth safe and hidden. Is my seven better than six? Are seven days mine too? Seven nights are the best, out on the mesa, all smells and footsteps, the creatures move together and keep the biggest rocks in place. I know a stone that was a tree before the sky fell on it.

'Don't run around in your bare feet. Remember the scorpions,' Nelly is saying.

And if enough stones crumble, if the sky falls on Nelly

there will be no more names of things. Nelly writes her name on everything and calls it a lesson. Papa says fine – why should I learn what everyone learns? When the time comes, he says, I will know everything. I wonder about that, and about Papa. I think I don't like him. Maybe. But he is Papa.

'They aren't bare. My socks are still on,' Destina pulls at Nelly. 'Take my socks off, then.'

Nelly is looking out the window. 'Take them off yourself.'

What can Nelly see from that window if she doesn't even know what to look for? She can't see those eyes coming straight at me when I think of my friend. How he lifts his paw to my shoulder when I ask him to say what he means. He might really tell me next time. And next time is now, now, now.

Destina moved to her bed and without undressing climbed into it. That way, Nelly would leave. And so she did, picking up the dust-reddened socks, the slippers, half closing the door behind her as she went. Lying now in the high room the child stares at nothing, for behind her eyes is another home to go to. Her hand flips at the tassels on the bed curtain, making them swing away and back, the longest brushing her cheek on its wide arc over the pillows. In that secret home there is Albert, Albert is back, sitting there ready to eat for her, dance for her, be her friend, take her to his rivers and waterfalls and towns with elevators. 'Now I have two friends.'

Could anyone presume to discover her truth – even with probing? It would be no surprise if the prodigal gloom of the big house with its dark stairs and heavy walls had quelled the child's spirit. But children don't perceive ugliness. No matter how dreary or squalid the surroundings, a child's mood is not affected, pervaded as it is by the compulsive life force and a triumphant aimless optimism. From the tender strands of Destina's childish wonder she weaves a tapestry as fragile as spider silk, adequate to her needs. She gazes at the world with trust, a trust just barely colored with wariness. She doesn't hate, only repudiates, while her passionate soul waits like a rudderless little boat for a strong wind. And if her fire smoulders underneath an unlit quotidian, it also lights her way to escape.

Destina lived wholly in this child's world. Life at Windcote encroached hardly at all on her secret sphere. She had few human contacts: Nelly, her papa, and the servants. Nelly, who seemed never to have been a child at all but to have sprung, obtuse, stolid, bovine, from some weedy pasture, was her most urgent impediment. Meridian, though he sat with her sometimes, or rode with her on the windy plain, talked always in strangely exalted phrases that she didn't understand or even listen to, preferring the chorus of voices that came from sand and scrub on palo-verde hills. She heard how buzzards stirred up the sky with their caws and sent squirrels streaking behind the ocotillos. The rides would often end abruptly when Meridian, unnerved by these signs of raw life – the occasional gila monster or coiled snake – turned his horse and ordered the girl to follow him, though more often than not she went on alone. In the big house Indian servants were taciturn and kept their distance, a manner natural to them in their dealings with the invader, and in this case heightened by certain instructions from their master.

Though Nelly was indeed a nuisance, even her attentions were of a casual, desultory nature. Destina easily triumphed over her governess in almost every clash of will, that quality flickering in Nelly with such a feeble glow as to be virtually absent. Moreover, the closeness and monotony of their days together had resulted in a graceless familiarity that belied the relationship of governess and pupil, making it easy for the girl to have her way. Never having clung to the bosom of a mother, she had an independence of spirit that would have confounded far more lively intelligences than that of the wretched Nelly. If her manner was naive, her intensity was not.

For an hour Albert Exodus had seen that intensity in the depths of her clear gaze. He had been shown the treasure of her memory box. She had also shown him her violence, her fragility, and something else, a kind of torch that shone like a prospect of rescue. Did she receive something in return? Did this slender young man with the pale narrow face and pointed beard, his obliging appetite, his talk of blackmail, brand on her spirit a comparable mark? Whatever he was, she trusted him. With that quick certainty of a child's judgment, she knew from his gaze and the sound of his voice that he was not among the enemy.

Night surrounds her now, warm and ozone-laden. Windows are open to that pungency that reaches the nose like an invitation to levitate. The curtains move now and again as if to bring the sage and dust and even the sky into the room. The only sound is the quick, level whisper, like the rustlings of sleepy birds, of Destina on her bed.

'Come out! Come out! The blackmail is dancing on its one thousand feet. Nelly has no blackmail, she is a fee-mail, Papa calls her fee-mail. There's blackmail in the tamarisk tree, hiding with a black spider who stuck it there – every night it thinks up stories down at the foot of Los Lobos Rock. Tonight I'll meet my friend there; he knows where those two are hiding. They are all hiding; everyone in the canyon is hiding from blackmail. Knock, knock, let me in. There are big houses inside of me, full of blackmail, ready to pounce. Albert and Miss Blackmail will sit down and talk things over, and he'll say, Destina, you were right, blackmail is truly good for you. That's when blackmail will start growing bigger and blacker. It will fill up the town and the sky so that everything is black, black, black, black. If you don't believe me just ask my friend, he isn't afraid of anything, not even blackmail, blackmail . . . '

Pushing back the pillows the girl swung her feet to the floor and slid down from the bed. She waited there, listening, then picked her way across the room through the tangle of objects, coming to the window where she dropped down to lean on the sill.

'Oh Albert, I have to go out to my other friend, I promised him this afternoon. You won't mind when I show you.' Kneeling there at the window she might have been any child saying its prayers, looking into the starry void, asking for safekeeping and confident that it would be granted. The May night was already riding with the moon and her tattered veils over dunes and distant cliffs. It was out there that her friend was waiting. Patiently? Or with lonely thoughts and nothing to do, watching the moon alone? But she would tell him about Albert. How he left Nelly standing there, how he so kindly ate her dinner. Would her friend like Albert? He *was* her friend, but like Papa he watched her, maybe he wanted her to stay as she was.

Yet why shouldn't she like Albert? And she wondered, 'Can Albert dance on a rope and catch snakes? Nelly can't dance at all, she only sits and sways in her chair and is crazy afraid of lightning. Besides, she is so dumb and spongy when she looks at Papa. Oh, my friend, why are you alone in the desert, why don't you live here with me instead of Nelly?'

Down in the corral a horse neighed, and the sound came to the window like a summons. Destina slid down from the bed and ran over to an oak wardrobe. Pulling out a pair of boots she drew them on, her face crossed with faint light,

86

intent and serene. She raised the lid of a chest at the foot of her bed, took out a chunk of meat, and stuffed it into a handbag. Swinging the handbag, she opened the door, listened, then walked through the outer room, weaving through the wilderness of furniture. That door too she opened, listened again to the furry silence, stepped into the corridor, closed the door behind her and hurried down the hall to the stairs.

7

Crouched in the ravine beyond the stable, his back resting against the rise that hid him from the house, Albert struck a match and lit a cigarette. He held the match down to his watch. Twenty-three minutes to one. A flicker of air blew out the match in his hand, yet he held it there, listening to the sounds that hovered about the house: sudden laughter, a door closing, a gasp of music. His hand trembled slightly. He had arranged everything with perfect calm, the horses stood tethered near, their flanks gleamed and rippled in faint light as they pawed the ground, saddle leather sibilant, nostrils lifted to the wind, expectant, curious. He had been efficient, even nerveless. Yet he felt now a momentum, his blood surging against his temples in a kind of roar, as the wheels of this night's agenda that he himself had set in motion were spinning without him.

A sudden fountain of rage suffused him, impotent and foredoomed. Then, as suddenly, he was quiet with recognition – of the lusterless amalgam of events, the ache of expecting a peace that would never be his. His undistinguished existence was spread out before him like used clothes. In those early years he had been so sure of turning the stream of his awareness into some sort of creation, something that would be his. During countless hours the pressure of ennui pulverized every seed of thought while he fought the whisper: nothing is worth it. With every new try it came: nothing I do can ever make any difference. And finally, crushingly, that moment of lonely clarity when he said, nothing is my name.

Since then he wandered. He did what was asked of him, he gratified in some measure his senses. The world was crumbling, but he didn't blame the world. There was no one to blame. Inconspicuous and observant as he was, the ambitions of people distressed him. That they persisted in their goals struck him as insipid. Greed or charity, it was all the same, all tainted, all useless. Then he was a critic? 'You do not become a critic,' Gautier once said, 'until it has been completely established to your own satisfaction that you cannot be a poet.'

One thing seemed to carry him along: his love of women. Their volatile charms, their pretty colors, their talent for making time pass painlessly had brought him often into their auras and their beds. So when he found Nadine Coussay he came to think of marriage and a permanent companion, all to the conforming good. Beautiful as she was, she had given him pleasure in his role of lover and protector, even though protection was not exactly what she would have called her need.

It was all so remote now. And weakly drawn. The fabric of that role lay before him, comical, pathetic, and in pieces like some battered backdrop in an empty theater – Nadine too a dim painted image, the whole picture a bad copy, cherubs with the faces of old boys and their hands turned around, self-conscious vistas, impossible perspectives, all gleefully brushed and impossible. And now, on top of it all, peeling.

He heard steps in the direction of the stable, light running steps and the sound of a gate swinging out and banging closed. He moved to stand up but stopped and sat back on the rocks. Why show himself? Nadine would come; she knew where he was. He inhaled on the cigarette, its tip close to his watch. Eighteen minutes to one. Then she was indeed prompt. He waited, crushed the stub in the sand, his ears straining toward the sounds. What was she doing? If this was some new kind of game . . .

But on these thoughts came the sudden clatter of hooves, uneven, cavorting, then the firm staccato beat of a full gallop. Albert sprang up. His glance scaled the arroyo wall and thrust over its edge into the sky, quivering in the vastness for a shocked second, then rebounding back with no answer to his brain. He flung himself against the rocky abutment, scrabbling up its side on all fours, his eyes reaching ground and landscape. It was all over in a moment. Pounding hooves swept close, a phantom form carved with mane and tail and fluttering white, a face swooping near, swooping in and away. Fading, then, as the very air shuddered, leaving an image seared on his eyes like a flashed light. Albert's fingers loosened on the rocks as his body slid down the slanted wall. His lips formed a word, a name: Destina.

Again he lay against the wall hearing only hoofbeats and the sound of his heart. He felt no surprise, only awe for the accuracy of an event he had only guessed at. Moonlight wove the landscape into a web of icy pallor.

The two horses pawed the gravel, theirs heads flung up, tense and inquiring. Albert began lighting another cigarette, knowing the girl would come, feeling her near, he heard her there. Twelve minutes to one. In the same moment a light step, a leaping down, and beside him her small flat voice, 'Well, Albert.'

She stood over him, running a pocket comb through her hair. Hung about her neck and waist were binoculars as well as a movie camera for hand-held filming. Its long black snout rocked on her stomach and made him think of the mariner's albatross though less beautiful. How like Nadine, he mused, to burden herself with the wrong things, the impractical tourist preparing for the guided tour. He watched her adjust a strap. 'Cigarette?' He held out the packet.

'Not now, thanks. What are we waiting for?'

'Why, nothing, really.' He observed her casual air and asked, 'Are you on a tight schedule?'

'Maybe I am. What of it? In any case I didn't come out here to smoke.'

'No. Of course.' He stood up, brushing away the sand. 'I'm not quite sure what you did come for.'

Though she didn't suspect anything so unsure in herself, Nadine didn't know either. Nor why she had made this rendezvous at all, since she had accepted that morning to spend the evening with her host who would show her through his laboratory. Indeed, it had begun as planned. He had conducted her to this tightly closed place, had shown her one or two of its wonders, when she felt a peculiar hesitance. It was all so odd – and airless seeming. With a murmured excuse, something about 'just for a moment' she left the room. It needed time, this sort of thing. Seeing the animal, the lion, would give it all a focus, a clearer reason for all these actions, with their motives in plain view. Fifteen minutes later she found herself down at the stable, in boots, with camera and binoculars.

'Oh, I'm well aware of your new self,' Albert went on, 'but I'm not interested. I'm even amazed at our empty past. You see, I've changed too.'

'Yes – I've noticed.' She dragged it out, really looking at him now.

'Noticed? That I'm not lost, bewildered, suffering? That must be disconcerting for a woman.'

92

'Why woman? Anyhow it's just as well. Who is the new love? The place certainly abounds in candidates.'

He laughed a little. 'You amuse me with that. Anyway, let's go, Nadine. That is, if you're still on.' He untethered the horses. 'And by the way, you won't need the camera, there simply isn't enough light.'

Nadine said nothing. She waited while he untied the bridles and handed her one. They swung into their saddles. Nadine's stirrup had to be shortened, and Albert bent to adjust it. Looking at the toe of her boot, his fingers were suddenly awkward, as he fumbled for the buckle, thinking about how the toe, the boot, and, inside, the foot he knew so well was no more to him now than the bronze foot of a statue.

They walked the horses up the dry wash, heard hooves slipping among loose stones, clatter of stones, neighs of horses, sibilant leather, until they came out on open ground.

'We're taking the trail to the canyon. I checked it this afternoon. It's fairly smooth for the first three miles.'

'All the better,' said the girl as she kicked her mount firmly in the flank. The animal trotted out in a level canter. Albert's horse, taking the sign, sprang too.

Soon Windcote was far behind; its windows staring in moonlit discontent at a landscape that would never be theirs, its imported tropical birds murmuring in their cages, its master grimly searching for the one golden bird that had flown. Nadine.

8

He began by moving through the house at his usual pace, deliberate, heavy, assured, with only the very slightest interruption of step from time to time, stopping short as if a fly had buzzed across his face and had to be brushed away before he could proceed. Each room, questioned, gave back the question with a shrug: the salon, the dining room, a string of featureless 'game' rooms, the echoing hall where he went quickly to the staircase, climbing its steps in that confident way a blind man will walk to show you he knows where he is going. A clock struck two. Meridian swayed through the second-floor corridor, came to Nadine's room, and threw the door wide. It was dark and empty. A glance inside, he turned and, uncertainly now, went back to the corridor. He kept waving away the motes shimmering in the spaces between wall lamps. Of course Albert's room was empty; it looked as if no one had ever been there.

He came finally to the terrace, crossing it in a zigzag path, southeast to its opposite side, and again across its surface several times that brought him to the aviary at the southwest corner of Windcote's massive bulk. He looked around him, remembering with a razor clarity the scene of only two hours earlier: his guests playing at identifying constellations to the sounds of guitar strumming, while the night wind came up; Nadine insisting on the superiority of Louisiana stars, accepting the shawl he brought; Nadine not accepting Vine's élan as he laughed and said these are the same stars, while Ritter was not so sure – there was something about the way the planet turned, there was something too about the girl's perception of stars; and Chichi shrugging, turning to Maya in genuine astonishment at these weirdoes talking about stars like little babies.

Now the house was asleep behind its closed doors but she was not there. When had she gone? They had been so close, so breathingly near, her back so yielding as he pushed her down into the leather and steel of his favorite … no, no, no, no. He was getting ahead of himself, it had not happened, but it would happen, she was there at Windcote this very night to justify his power and ingenuity. He would see her beauty dissolve and spread like opalescence, and her pristine consciousness spinning, abject …

Meridian half saw these events in his present fever. Annoyance had long since given way to distraction, conscious and sharp. He had felt in the last hour two or three of those little seismic vibrations that herald a serious interruption of pleasure. So when he found himself alone on the terrace with a cageful of birds he began talking to himself, in a low tone, with fluttering hands and a shaking of the head as if in some denial. Night blades of sage-laden wind sliced at his face without affecting its swoon. His flailing arms came against the cage bars, shook them and swore in fury at the cacophony of tiny protests. Spinning round with the apparent weightlessness peculiar to certain heavy persons, he floated across to the parapet, leaning there in mute rage, demanding of the indifferent dark: he ran back to the house wall, sliding his big body toward the glass doors through which, like a clumsy marauder, he cast sly urgent glances into his own rooms. Pulling aside the door he passed inside, only to confront once more the foolishness of his furniture, the cozy divans holding no one, the lamplight illuminating nothing. There was a kind of voluptuousness about his present suffering, an emanation of the exquisite that, to a specialist in these matters, could have been described as aura.

His breathing labored, this searching was already fully orgasmic, the prologue to a fainting. He seemed not to see at all. The deep pouches overhung with folds of lids, blankets for his straining eyes, already made seeing a reptilian exercise. Light only drove him frantic. Bumbling, he whirled and whirred in his moth-gray velvet raiment. Nadine.

Staggering again through the house, moaning her name, his face was gutted with frenzy. Upstairs, lurching to the south tower, he passed several doors of his sleeping guests, came to a closed stairway, almost fell on the little steps, and threw the door wide – and as quickly stumbled away, his sight tangled in a flash of tan skin and white, a tight weave of curving bodies in a need as alien to him as the breeding antics of his horses. No matter. She was not there. She was not anywhere. Over and over he asked himself the same whimpering questions like a child. What had happened? Why had she left? Wasn't she happy in the laboratory? It had begun so marvelously well. Oh, she was hiding, teasing him, playing a game. She would come out; she would not spoil his wonderful night . . .

Hands reaching wide, flicking the walls, he went through another corridor to his own wing and leaned finally against his own door, forehead pressed to the panel, fingers clutching the knob. He stood there a while, sagging on cool wood, gasping the words: Come back, come back, come back, my little bitch . . .

Something soft, a warm breathing mass, came then, rustling near the floor and laid itself trembling and without sound along his leg. Wild relief leapt in him and he curved down to clasp the huddled figure. 'Nadine, Nadine,' his thickened tongue found no other words. As he whispered his hands moved ever more knowingly, ever more quiet with recognition, the name glued to his lips, his gentle clasping become a vise. With one foot he pushed the door. White light fell where he stood, and the face at his feet looked up, like the face of a animal that knows only the drag of its own longing. Abject, insistent, Nelly crouched there, a sharply drawn image that breathed and uneasily smiled. When he turned and went in she rose to follow him. They stood just inside the door, Meridian swelling with rage, the girl patient, doglike. He stepped carefully forward and brought his hand around in a heavy swing to the side of her head, toppling her sideways, her arms half lifted like a jointed toy. As she struck the floor one muffled groan escaped her stretched lips, one sound only, and from where she lay her square fawning gaze clung to the man's face. A little blood trickled from the left side of her mouth. Soon she began to rise, ponderously, bracing her body on a chair. He watched her, his face twitching. Then he stepped close again, lifted his foot, and sent her knotted figure sprawling on the carpet. This time she did not get up but lay where she had fallen, the blood smeared on her chin, her smile fixed and obscene, her eyes half closed. He stood there wavering for a moment, then veered back toward the open door and ran from the room.

9

Nelly, waking, rolled over on her back and opened her eyes. She had no idea how long she had been lying on this floor in the apartments Meridian called his laboratory. She was coming to slowly, though her right eye was blurred, her chin felt wet and sticky, and there was a pain in her side. Oh, what of it! She knew the room by heart and only waited for the mirrors and apparatuses to stop heaving and flashing so she could somehow sit up, which she soon did by catching hold of a leather horse's steel hoof. Light from one lamp dusted the room's contents just enough to show her where she was. Her first thought, first imperative: the head scarf that lay on the floor just out of reach. She rocked and dragged herself to grab it, tie it on, hide her head, hide the hair so unevenly chopped, her scalp showing pale between tufts. Whether she remembered the encounter – of how long before? – or whether it would affect the way she negotiated the rest of the night, were questions as foggy as the mind that played with them, the mind that formulated out of a kinetic confusion of images one immediate need: to get to her room. She pulled herself up and tottered out to the hall. A kind of blunt homing instinct took her through the sleeping house – how late was it, how late could it be? – and to the stairway. She didn't stumble, didn't drag, but moved slowly up to her third floor.

Looking around at nothing in the almost total dark, Nelly asked the void: 'Who is she?' It was not a question so much as an acknowledgment of something, something that had been growing in her since yesterday, like a creature. It had nitched into her head and was moving through her body now, pouring its hordes and vapors and emanations on the placid water that was Nelly's being. She didn't know what to do with it. Nothing had prepared her for anything so closely resembling an emotion. Her recent battering, far short of mutilation and fading steadily as she went up the stairs, provoked not the slightest consideration, save as an ordained necessity. That her mouth was bleeding, that she swallowed blood, that it tasted pleasantly salty were mere sensations, with no particular messages to her brain. It was all in the way of things. But this time was different. An outline of cause, overarching, bringing her confusion into a state of near terror, clung to her mind as she fumbled for the big key.

Without turning on the lamp she lay down on her bed, impervious to a jutting driftwood stem that poked at her back. She had wiped the blood from her chin and, in general, felt bodily whole, but everything was now wrapped in fog. For the something, the insidious thing that ate at her composure as if it would destroy her entirely, still burned in her head and her chest. It would have to go away. It would have to be dealt with. Nelly lay there quietly, eyes open on the dark. During those hours the earth turned ever so slightly, and as the time passed under her disarray, night had begun its lurching transformation into day.

So Nelly too lurched to her feet and, foraging in the chest of drawers, found what she was looking for, tucked it in her skirt, and stood for a while at the window. Outside, the landscape was emerging as if from the developing bath of the darkroom. Dunes and hills flowed away in watery imitation of land. It was that hour of dawn when the earth is remote and unreliable, especially to Nelly looking at nothing in particular. For her, sand wasn't really sand unless it got in your shoes, and if it blew from mesa floor to dry gully to hills and finally to the infested canyon it only meant you were better off in the house where nothing moved without permission. Along the line that separated desert from cliffs, an undulating ridge moved, left to right; two tamarisk trees shook their feathers in the morning wind; and, yawning, she could see the gashed pink dune where among tumbled rocks had lain those remnants of driftwood (they had never drifted) that decorated her room and her inconsequence.

When she turned away, everything now awash in palest

light, she wasn't doing any thinking. In fact, she didn't know much about thinking. Drab as were the events of her short life, no thinking part of it had ever been hers; it was an area of activity always performed by others, like warning and lecturing and punishing, all in the exercise of some muggy precepts and all, she had lately been assured, having nothing to do with her. Nothing had ever pointed to thinking as a habit to get into, and as for any effect it might have on her fate, well, there would always be someone, there *was* someone, she firmly believed, to do it for her.

It was still dark in the corridors, but she knew their meanders. Swaying, she went down the stairs and through another hall directly to the room that had been assigned to Nadine. There she waited and listened. A natural thing to do, listening, like an animal or a bird, one of those little desert listeners outside under the sky, always on the alert. But then she pushed the door, looked inside. Nadine was not there.

It would be anyone's fantasy, and only fantasy, to imagine what Nelly would have said to Nadine, asked Nadine, done to Nadine had Nadine been in her room, had perhaps gone to bed with the door unlocked – necessarily, for there were no locks – had, waking, rubbed her eyes, slowly sensing a stolid figure standing over her, a half-seen presence that at this unseemly hour could not have been friendly. And still fantasizing, one could make Nadine suddenly very clever and wily, the way some people are when in doubt, or in downright danger? 'Hi! Oh – could you wait a minute while I go to the bathroom . . .' slipping from the sheets and darting, very fast, to the bathroom door – and a lock. So would this night at Windcote have had a different ending, just as all nights, everywhere, choose their own endings, with or without nightwalkers and their fantasies.

But as Nadine was not in her room it was all so different. So very different for Nelly, who, flinging the door wide and moving across the gravely lighted space, found the bed. On it lay Meridian – or rather curled, for his big knees were pulled up to his belly, his arms wrapped around a pillow, his face hidden. He was crying. Muffled whimpers came from under the pillow, those strangely childish sounds a big man can make in extremity, whether from pain or ecstasy.

Nelly's eyes gazed. Though her awareness of the scene before her was actual and palpable, rational consideration of it was impossible. She didn't ask herself useless questions, such as how Meridian had come to be on this bed, where had he taken off most of his clothes, how had he managed to entangle his flesh in these brown rags that seemed to wind erratically around his sweating body like vines. She saw it all as a picture badly drawn, but a picture that should never have been painted, that could not have been painted, must not ever be painted. Blunt hammers in her head pounded out an iron warning to her certainty. Had she understood, it would have rung as clear as tolling bells: the litany of her 'education' and its precepts that had not only sustained her but had literally created her out of a mass of girlish putty found obediently breathing in a correctional home. The years – five of them had passed since her arrival – of total and contented submission to the master of Windcote were now all she knew. It was the shape of her consciousness, such as it was: the putty had hardened into a chunky dull-skinned form that could withstand all imaginable assaults of physical pain and/or pleasure, simply because it seemed to have no soul and no apparent desire to possess one. Souls, said Meridian, made him laugh. He could see them knocking about like tied-up parcels in the wind, to be shipped off to heaven when their owners tired of them or died. He had poured into Nelly's ears a thousand bits of information or sophistry of this kind, divulgings of secret wisdom not given, he said, to just anyone; in this way literally giving her life while sharing it in indescribable ways she adored. He had regularly brought her to flaming orgasm, a thing she had come to think of as life itself. The spaces of time between them, the sounds and sights around them, and the biological needs of the body, such as eating and sleeping, counted as nothingness.

Crude and powerful repository of wisdom and breath-taking secrets, Meridian was thus master not only of Windcote but of bliss. She had seen him in all his guises. She had watched him with others, with his child. But until yesterday nothing and no one had burst in to menace her glistening existence. Though he might bring in an occasional friend, or friends – always grudgingly accepted by Nelly – to join them in the laboratory, nothing had come to waken her from her contented coma, no one to threaten her sovereign life.

She looked down at him now as she heard him moan the name. He lay there on the rumpled sheet, resembling one of those gigantic freaks of vegetable growth – a gourd, a potato, a melon? – people love to display from their gardens. He may have sensed Nelly's presence standing near, but only pleaded the name from the depth of his pillow, in a high bubbling voice: 'Nadine!' At each utterance Nelly trembled; night flowed back into the room like sticky tar, engulfing her in a bitter darkness. She felt herself hurtling backward into that long-ago desolation of the orphans' home. Meridian's moans and whimpers burned like matches before her eyes, yellow flashes that studded the space between her and his grief. To stop them she leaned over him, daring to say the words she knew now were the wrong ones.

'It's me. Nelly. I want to help you.'

He pulled his blotched, tear-stained face from the pillow to look at her. They were eye-to-eye in the off-white light of dawn. Although he stared unseeing, his expression resembled the pout of a naughty child. In the throes of obvious delirium he did not flinch at Nelly's flat voice, nor was there any move to send her away. He was in that state of the sufferer who, no matter how imperious and difficult in health, is, when ailing, suddenly humble and grateful for the least solace. Nelly was vaguely aware of this exchange of places and filled her new role with resolute energy, in spite of the hammer in her head brought on by his raving. Two or three elements in the present situation were as clear to her as the advancing daylight: there would be no problem with Meridian – he was at this moment completely in her hands; she must help him stop calling, stop those awful reminders of whom he wanted. Maybe if Nadine were to appear beside the bed he would not recognize her. Let her appear! Let her take one quick look while there was time. Let her see him and go away, for he would not need her any more, in this room, in the laboratory, or anywhere else.

All this time Nelly was soothing her wrecked god, stroking his brow, wiping his frothed mouth, adjusting his burlap bonds. 'It's all right, now. We can pretend,' she whispered. 'We *are* in the laboratory, aren't we now?'

Meridian rolled his eyes around without, of course, seeing anything. But he responded in that docile way of a four-year-old who's been bribed with a cookie. 'Yes. Yes.'

'And we'll play our best game, right? I'll be Nadine.'

'Yes. Oh, yes.' Like a trained elephant he lifted his two fat arms to rest them against the brass bars of the bedstead while Nelly picked up from among the rags on the floor two long burlap bands and tied his wrists to the bars. It was a familiar routine. Writhing and undulating while the same procedure attached his feet to the bed – delicious preface to the game – he nevertheless began again talking to his dream.

Abruptly, Nelly turned away, went to the window. Down in the driveway idled the waiting car, and, as she watched, four heads equipped with bodies and overnight bags clambered into it. She might have been looking at a silent film for all the sound they made. The car soon disappeared in the dust. One thing she saw: Nadine was not among the passengers.

She came back to the bed and stood over Meridian. Looking down at his twisting and slavering, hearing his whining of the odious name, it seemed to her that he no longer had an identity at all. Who it was, what it was, were just more questions to mock her. She studied the mucid cavern of his mouth as it opened to swallow the world, this purple grotto emitting sound. And the hole in his belly – it was only a navel but it too was whispering, would be wanting something from her any minute now, another hole, maybe fluids. Longing for quiet, she drew out from her skirts the ice pick, and grasping it with both hands brought it down at the center of his big neck, and as soon pulled it out, releasing a tiny red jet like a toy fountain. The face on the pillow contorted, a gagged cry, more like a growl, held the mouth open while a violent reflexive spasm nearly tore him from his bonds. He might have been in the dentist's chair save for the rivulets of blood winding their way around the curve of his neck and soaking in under his head. Carried far away now, Nelly raised the instrument again. More fountains, more spurts of fountains bubbled up as she plunged her weapon again and again in the waxy flesh, in the chest, the stomach, the eye, the mouth, even a thigh when it flexed. Nelly was by this time thoroughly disgusted – she had not imagined provoking such hideous sounds.

After a while – time had no place in that event – the great hulk had finished its spasms and its crazy breathing. There was a great deal of blood. It reddened not only the bed, the carpet, the wall, but Nelly herself, who with the same energy swabbed at her shirt and face where drops had landed like warm spring rain. She did not touch him. There was no reason to – it wouldn't make him look better, it wouldn't even wake him up. Aware for the first time of her own presence, her strong arms, her power, she was yet conscious of some fathomless space inside her that needed definition. A something for Nelly to cope with, some words – but then, why struggle with words, she who had never learned them and didn't need them now? Tired and hot, she pulled up a chair as one does to sit beside the sick. Quiet, with her hands folded in her lap, she watched the progress of her work, the bubbling down of her little fountains settling to a steady ooze of deepening red, while a gray-green pallor spread already over the wreckage. So the time passed, trancelike and vehement. A ray of first sunlight touched the top of her head like a halo.

10

The trail to the canyon unrolled in two deep tracks rutted with the imprints of wagon wheels and hooves. Where it narrowed to a path the two horses slowed to a walk. Albert drew abreast of his companion. Out of his elation arose an impulse to say something pleasant to the girl, some easy phrase to allay her tension and win a measure of confidence, though he wanted it for her sake rather than his own. She looked tense and almost sad, her face rigidly forward, her posture stiff and unyielding to the horse beneath her. Yet, staring ahead, it was she who spoke.

'You're bristling with questions, Albert. I can feel them ticking. But keep them. They'll just bounce. I'm simply not answering.'

Albert gazed at her. 'Come on, Nadine,' he said gently, 'we're not enemies, only rather stale friends. We just don't mix any longer, our chemistries have changed. It happened pretty suddenly but it happened. Maybe it isn't so regrettable.'

'Of course not. I, at least, have nothing to regret.'

'Not even your hair? It was so pretty.'

'Yes. And useless. Hanging on me. It's transformed now, it belongs to someone else. It has a different life since it left me. I'm even told it has powers – by someone who knows these things. What's hair after all? A symbol.' She recited her dicta like an apt pupil. Albert listened, amused.

'Possibly,' he said after a moment, 'it serves as a woman when the woman isn't there. Substitution. The disease of our time.'

'Disease? Isn't that just a point of view? Lots of things are called diseases. To city men like Ritter or Ralph Vine, nature is just sick. Who's going to separate the sick and the well?'

'You could say that the sick ones are out of touch with their world, cover their self-loathing with words—'

'Maybe I don't want to be healthy,' Nadine's voice rose, defiant.

'Then you'd better resign yourself, Nadine,' he said dryly. 'You are certainly among the well. Oh I understand what you want. Of course. You want to experience the uncommon, to push open all the doors. You are determined to know your own depths and,' he couldn't help adding, 'I suppose, a few highs. Nothing could be healthier. But, believe me, you're wasting your potential here. You're pushing against a door without hinges, no lock, no key, a fungoid door, if you want to know. Because you'll feel it turn to powder in your hand—'

'Please. I haven't asked any questions. So spare me the answers. It's obvious you're prejudiced. So it's my turn to *understand* something. You're prejudiced by the circumstances—'

'Wrong again. It's just these circumstances that have given me new eyes.' Merely to hear his own voice made his heart turn in his chest. He looked at her. 'I pity you, Nadine. I pity you because you're doomed to disappointment and despair. That sound portentous? Do you think I don't know what you're looking for, hoping for? Maybe you don't know what a beaten path you're setting out on. Thousands have been there before you. What is it now but a tourist trap? About as far from true adventure as a mudbath.'

'Is this ride an adventure or a mudbath?'

'I'm not sure.' Albert was suddenly quiet as their horses walked through the wash, hooves slipping on the rubble of stones. 'Here I am pontificating again,' he reminded himself. 'How disgusting! I'm not even sure why I say these things to a girl who should be left alone to bruise her life in her own way. After all, advice is a dreary part of any exchange, and as boring.' How could he hold up to her his own years, twelve of them seeming like fifty, full of nothing but revolt without any conclusions or even peaceful rest. No, since they had given him nothing but deeper bafflement, how could their failure warn this beautiful but mistaken girl? His thoughts sank into gloom as a torrent of ugly memories mounted in him like nausea. They tore along at the level of his eyes in a mocking procession, as sharply visible as pictures on a screen. Mudbath indeed!

He noticed that his mind was running on two tracks at once. For if the new euphoria of being at Windcote was initiated by Nadine, who, after all, had led him here, the other world he had found in this same mansion denied her very existence, calling to him alone from its charmed evanescence. He had lunged often enough at deceitful doors only to drag himself away each time like a wounded animal. Now, beyond this open door, he thought he recognized a tender answer: the reality of Destina, a child. In her he believed he saw his salvation.

It was the absolute certainty of Destina's rendezvous with her 'friend' that led Albert to penetrate these uneasy crags in the middle of the night with a naturalist who wanted to see, not to understand. It didn't matter. Because he too needed to see as a further step in his own involvement, his longing for a crystalline music of simple truths – all so terribly far from those antic signposts that had seen him move crazily from one wrong address to another ... Mrs Harrison's Furnished Lodgings for Gentlemen, a place and time impossible to equate with the present, so contrasted that his mind shrank in its snail shell at the very thought of those scenes. Saigon, was it? Or Bangkok? 'Young man not happy? Come, one try twenty yuan.' Rickshaw boys laughing in their sleeves, pointing at his gloomy face. 'Once more, two yuan.' He had gone on, moving like so many others, under the delusion that constant change of place, not pace, brings answers not to be found at home.

In their frame of joss house and silk shop, Mrs Harrison's rooms for gentlemen wait for evening as Mrs Harrison sits on the stoop and babbles to her listless dog. Reek of disinfectant on crochet and frayed wicker, Mrs Harrison in the doorway, an apparition of ruin sidling near.

'May I come in, Mr Exodus, I've brought some tea,' her genteel voice rasping like a worn phonograph record, dainty, arch. 'You don't sleep, Mr Exodus? Too high-strung for this heat. I don't sleep either. I worry about my young men, alone in this wicked city. Oh my, if you only knew, dear boy, if you only knew—'

A hand fluttering on his sleeve, scandalized click of the tongue, her orange hair and lace shawl wrapping Albert in the choking drift of the exhumed. The other side of the world and yet not so different from Finlay's Mortuary and Joe, who worked for Finlay without pay: 'Come on, Albert, before the others get here.' Gray voices trembling on the phone, night arrivals, commotion of doors. Devoid of substance they satisfied their putrescent need, ravishers more deathbound than the ravished. And Joe, funny Joe, who wasn't so funny after all.

Albert stared ahead, grateful to be in Destina's canyon, for he knew it was hers. He knew in the most wonderful way that she was not far, and that he would see her friend.

The horses were entering a ravine wide enough for the two riders to move side-by-side, but they needed urging, the dark was deeper there. They balked and tossed their manes, stumbled on flint and stones.

Sitting stiffly in the saddle, Nadine talked on. 'Maybe we are all following the same will-o-the-wisp,' she said. In the narrow corridor of stone her words came crashing back to him, hollow echoes – *isp, isp, isp* – 'But I have my own method' – *method, method, method* . . .

A soft wind had come up, pushing her sorry clichés in his face like tumbleweed. Will-o-the-wisp! Method! Why try to warn her now? Beautiful Nadine, spinning out an ever more fragile thread. She will not recognize her own delusion even when it is too late.

Offended at his guessing, she would refuse to admit that his life in any way resembled the adventure she believed was calling to her alone. Could it be, Albert mused, that we exalt daring in ourselves and despise it in others? The one unbearable fact – that many have done it before. The kind of searching made so famous (and now so available) by those who had sung their cadenced histories to the world would soon be obsolete, a game as quaint and as nostalgic as the regular reappearance of modes of dress. He felt the present as sullen, swinging like a pendulum against them both as they faced their separate choices. And in the blowing sand he breathed a secret fragrance: Destina. Could anything else save him now?

The trail had narrowed to a footpath and began its gradual ascent along the cliff shelf. Slowing, the horses leaned in from the void to their left. Albert rode ahead. At once shielding and hostile, the tall buttes reared in layered striations on the opposite side. Horses and riders pressed close to the rock wall, their hands reached out to touch the cool, somehow reassuring shale. Outlines gouged themselves into the blue air like acid-etched lines on copper, while the round indifferent moon moved behind a cloud like an unreliable friend.

Nadine reined in her horse. In the hollow dark only the rapping, slipping hooves and the deepening opacity of the shadows showed her the moving figure before her. Her petulant words echoed back to her.

With an effort Albert recalled his mind from its plunge. In truth, he had lost all interest in keeping up a conversation that was as futile as it was distasteful. He was amazed at what had happened to the girl in little more than a day and a night. The sweet babble he had become used to had turned into a rote of tired platitudes sprinkled with pompous winks at nihilism. There was something unattractive and even a little embarrassing about the girl's dilemma. Her 'method', as she called it, was a delusion, her present foil a bloated ruin.

She seemed to want to talk about Meridian but Albert was as determined to avoid the subject. Meridian and his intrigues were now the merest speck on the horizon of his mind. After all, the man was a carbon copy of his kind, mercifully rare. Let him play with his ingenious harnesses of leather, his steel vises, his ornaments, his mechanized games, his elegant objects designed for the penetration of orifices. Everyone to his own devices, with hands trembling or steady, each to his own menu and *bon appétit*. If this girl believes she is doing something amazing it isn't for me to spoil her game. If indeed I could. But what is there to say?

In that moment, however, he was spared any need to reply, the trail having come abruptly to its end. They were now nearly a hundred feet over the precipice and the horses were standing on a little ledge, their heads nodding in patient bafflement.

'We dismount here.'

'Okay,' murmured the girl, adding, 'What awful blackness!'

In fact, the mineral dark had surrounded them at the same time as a purring sibilance that unnerved Nadine. She felt rather than heard these sounds, as if the very crags were breathing over them. An opened fan of cloud lifted from the western horizon and advanced, a black island to enfold the moon.

'Sorry about leaving the flashlight.' Albert tried for a light tone. 'I did think of it but the moon was clearly out when we left. And it gave enough light.' He said it again in a dreamy way, 'Plenty of light.'

They got down carefully. He felt along the wall for a

projection and found a Joshua trunk growing from the rock face. Here he led the horses, tethered bridles. Moving to the ledge he joined Nadine, lambent in her pale shirt, sitting on the ground. She had tied her camera to the saddle and kept only the binoculars.

'Well, Albert,' she said almost listlessly, 'since you are going to produce a lion I suppose you can also arrange for some light to see it by. Or is that beyond your powers?'

'Come, let's start walking,' was his only reply.

Nadine stood up. 'Walking? Where? Are we going far? This seems as good a place as any. Where else is there to go? And in this dark!'

'You'll have to leave that to me. We're too near the horses and the trail. This is not a vantage point. Come on. We can take it slowly. Just walk directly behind me.'

'We should have done this in daylight,' she muttered, following him. 'At least we would see something . . . anything.'

'The lion, these lions anyway, do their roaming in the dark. They use night for the getting of food. People are apt to use it for getting into trouble.' Albert wasn't sure whether he was talking or thinking.

'Then are we getting into trouble?'

'That depends on who we are. Of course, daytime is a safety net. But it tends to slip away in the dark. The concept, I mean. That's why we go to sleep at night, to save us from ourselves.'

Nadine pondered this for only the fewest of moments;

then, as if to put an end to it, 'You'd better know where you're going, is all I can say.'

They turned into a narrow crevice behind the ledge and began to climb, mounting from rock to boulder to rock, Albert sometimes reaching around to pull her up when the footing broke away in shales. In this way, intent on the effort, they moved on and up, in and out, silent except for the quick constraint of breathing and hearing the soft breaking away under their feet of the rock fragments that clattered down, it seemed endlessly, like fading whispers, to the canyon floor.

From time to time Albert stopped to check their position, map the terrain. He had not come this far before. Yet he believed that advancing a few hundred feet along the cliff wall would do it, would bring them to a position with a view of the opposite density, a vast further aspect of diminishing crags and the placid hills dotted with brush. There they would wait and watch.

'It all seems so useless, so impossible," Nadine's words were mixed up with hard breathing. 'A stupid waste of effort.' She bent to shake a stone from her boot, holding to the jutting rock. 'How will I see anything with no light, especially from this distance? No light at all. We could be surrounded by the ark's entire passenger list and not know it. Oh, damn!' Her free hand struggled with the boot.

Albert stooped to help her. They went on for some time in silence. The profundity of the night and its star-ridden latitudes oppressed the girl. But to Albert it lay mercifully on his turbulent thought, a curtain of black gauze thrown across the new opulence of his spirit. He didn't notice her exasperation and had little interest in the outcome of his promise; it was a promise and would therefore be kept. The certainty of it gave him pause, and a sensation of something like awe mixed with a shared volition. But whose? He felt himself to be moving through the design of some outside compulsion with no exit from the maze but the one that signaled fulfillment of its intention.

Would Nadine's eyes see the tawny, softly padding lion on the opposite plateau? Would it turn toward them an answering gaze, summing in its savage glare the foolish, cruel, blunder-prone human outline? He knew he needn't ask. The proposition was presented and its conclusion superbly foregone.

On foot now, they felt their way along the cliff's ragged face. A frosty brilliance sifted down from heaven's dome, alive with stars, planets, novae, so remote yet so near that starlight would have been a brittle word for the radiance that streamed from the velvet void and that palely lit Albert and Nadine. They stumbled on and came at last to the spot Albert had known he would find for their vigil. He stopped there before a shallow cave resembling – absurdly, he thought – a theater proscenium. Its smooth floor extended to form a narrow ledge over the ravine. The landscape beyond the interval stretched back into a fading distance, though the opposite hill showed faintly, solemn and complex, in its frame of pared rock.

'Is this it?' asked the girl.

'This is it. We can sit down now. There's nothing to do but wait.'

Yet they both remained standing, uneasy in the sullen quiet. Nadine paced the ledge, her gaze straining toward the reaches beyond the ravine.

'I feel we aren't wanted here,' she said. 'We disturb the currents. They don't like us and I don't like them. I'm sure this place resents us.'

'I don't think it cares. I mean the place – this one or any other. Some people think it's only our presence that make's the vision a reality – for their minds' peace, I might add.'

'Oh, if they believe it that doesn't make it true. How can such ideas have any effect?'

'Naturally,' said Albert, taking the question, turning it slowly as if it held its own answer. 'But there's got to be something to name it. Whatever it is. For me, phenomena just don't exist without names. The name, the word is what makes everything real. Anyway, that's only my opinion. Names pump life into nothingness. Give it color and light and dark, you name it.' He laughed at that. 'Why, look over there above that butte. A round light. Is it the moon? You see, for me it isn't the planet but the word. And it isn't light but where it falls, the places that drink it in, and the eyes that reflect it . . .'

Nadine looked up. The moon was driving free of its shawl of cloud. In a moment it had rocked clear and unveiled. Radiance, coldly white, suffused the cliffs and faraway hills.

'How nice!' she said, suddenly lighthearted. 'Did you do that, Albert?'

She balanced on the edge of the precipice, her voice eased by the light, tinged with relief. 'Anyway, it looks better now.' She laughed a little. 'Even pretty!'

Pretty? Why not, if it was her word for what was there in the glittering theater he had chosen for their vigil. He looked down at her sitting on the ground, her back to the rock wall. She was intent on the binoculars, twisting their parts like a toy, her head bent in a way that gave her an aspect of total helplessness.

What, exactly, had happened to Nadine, the girl who said things like 'fiancé' and 'house party' and who pulled up the sheet before making her announcements? How, after years of apparently innocent ideas about nature in its dangerous aspects, had she come to this place of total ambiguity on a simple invitation? How had she fallen under its spell so completely as to drop her clothes for a dubious disguise at dinner, spend every minute since their arrival away from her 'fiancé'? Above all, what were these sophisms she now spouted, so alien to her normal talk?

Albert hardly noticed. So much had happened to his own perspective. At this moment he would have had trouble believing his actions in that dusky dining room of only half a day earlier.

Surmise is conjecture and conjecture is notoriously unreliable. But there was fascination in Nadine's new persona. It was not, perhaps, related to mere danger. Had her inchoate longings hidden an unconscious need of something far deeper? Clearly, she had found it here, but that something slyly forgot to tell her that nature wasn't always the same thing as evil. Then evil was her true need? Conjecture again. How deeply do we want to dig around in Nadine's psyche while she sits on the ground struggling with her binoculars? Being at this hour out in the canyon under a canopy of nature's supremest wonder, hoping to see a wild animal before her, was by now simply a reflex, or – conjecture once more – a tease, by her absence, a little torture for the would-be captor.

She focused her binoculars. She sighed, she swore. Albert watched and for a moment his heart went out to her. A being as beautiful as the day and so pathetically wrong. A someone as lost as himself, the two of them whirling in separate spaces, out of control. If he could take her in his arms, lay her head on his shoulder like a child, her defiant pose dropped at last; he might say something gentle, something reassuring ... Ah! But what?

He turned away. They were silent for a time, until, binoculars ready, Nadine joined him on the ledge, breathing, balancing. Until, in the next moment she drew in her breath and pointed toward the hills. She didn't speak, just stood there pointing across the void.

'Look!' she finally managed. 'Albert!'

Albert, still gazing into the sky, turned at her urgent whisper. He came over to where she stood, looked in the direction of her pointing finger. His face was still, it was the color of the moon.

Crossing the sage-dotted hill walked the figure of a child. So small, white-clad, and clearly feminine, it gleamed like phosphorus in the cool light. She moved slowly, yet with seeming purpose. It was easy to make out the little figure, even without binoculars, and Nadine watched now without them. Albert stood beside her, yet apart, transfixed. Their stares followed the figure, her white effulgence, her resolute crossing of sand and hillock, moving between rocks as on a cardboard stage. From one hand dangled what appeared to be a woman's handbag.

Stunned by the wonder of the moment, the two watchers, mute on their promontory, hardly breathed. Their eyes followed the girl. Once she stopped and stood for a moment to scan the cliffs, her face lifted, something like a question in the expression of her posture.

Nadine fumbled with the binoculars, focusing on the figure. As if drawn, the child turned then and as her gaze rested briefly in the direction of those two across the chasm, it seemed to Albert that she smiled.

Nadine found her voice. 'Albert, look!' she began in a

rush of words. 'Am I dreaming? I *must* be dreaming! Do you see a little girl over there, *there* on the other side?'

Clattering words, bursting in on the moment like a shower of pebbles in a gossamer web, 'Can you see her too, Albert? Albert, I simply can't be—'

Like a strike, she felt a painful grip on her arm. This time she looked hard at his altered face.

'Hush,' he said between his teeth, not looking at her, only staring at the child on the hill.

Nadine pulled at her arm. 'But what's the matter, what are you—'

He tightened his grip and shook her a little. 'You must be quiet.' He let her go and moved away.

She bent her head, rubbing the bruised arm. Then she glanced up at him and her glance became a derision, her mouth drooping open. Without moving her head she looked again toward the white figure in the distance, then back at Albert. She stared into his ashen face. She had never seen him like this, ever. A first awareness of Albert as a tragic figure – she would have said 'loser' – was spreading in her, staining the glassy surface of her mind. It mocked her. Albert the doomed. He was suddenly so *nothing* ... His predicament struck her as a betrayal, his transfixed pose was an infirmity, absurd.

The canyon was close now, a stale blue-lit room in a play being written by its helpless actors. Exasperation overwhelmed Nadine, the girl who had polished all her consciousness to a high, if brittle, finish that didn't include smudges. She shoved her hands in her pockets, spilling words that broke against the cliffs. Her pretty-girl voice, flat and furious, 'Why? Why should I be quiet?'

He didn't answer. He only shuddered at her scarring of the canyon's silence. His eyes clung to the child, his body became rigid. The moment became minutes, an endless time of crystallizing truths, with all his questions resolved into one answer: this enormous space that contained one image, a white gleam, blue-white floating through tufts of sage, alone in a grave secret purpose. Walking in the feathered light and stamped on immensity's stone face, the little form gave to Albert the only dream he would ever need.

Nadine leaned around to put herself in front of his face. She examined his disarray. And as soon began talking again – at first as if to herself, in a tone that mounted, then to the man trembling there. Suspended, her voice reverberated in the canyon like a sudden and mortal infection. It bled into the airy void, tore at his ears and his eyes.

Like someone who has been away Albert turned to her. By now his face wore an insensate expression impossible to equate with the one she had thought she knew. He seemed to be struggling with a problem of recognition, hesitating, as a sleeper hesitates to return to the catastrophe from which his slumber has removed him. His lips moved without sound, and he raised one hand and laid it, palm flat, along his cheek.

'Wait,' he brought out. 'Wait until – her friend, I – please be quiet . . .'

'Ah! Then there *is* something. Something really peculiar. And I've a right to know what it is.'

'No right,' said Albert, but to himself. Then, suddenly present, 'No,' he told her. 'You mustn't—'

'Who is that child? If you know anything why can't we do something, call to her, go help her?' On and up her words flapped in the wind, pitching into his distress. 'A night of sheer absurdity! What a farce! You bring me all the way out here to see a lion, that was your promise, big words, big mystery, all very effective,' plashing and spurting, the words went on, rolled and echoed in the red caves. 'And instead of a lion, I have to look at a *person*. God help me, I'm just the victim of a show-off! You fake!'

Albert lifted his hand as if to push back her voice. His face was distorted, his lips pressed together. 'If you'll wait,' he said then, 'just wait. She will—'

'She'll what?' Screaming now, the girl splashed her indignation over him, a rain of words all spattering rage and disappointment. There was no mystery, there was only a man's caprice. There was no adventure, only a promise unkept, no lions or anything else to see, only a silly boast and a man in ignominious awe of a little child, a man empty of all potential. She saw the figure on the opposite hill as no more than a further irritation, eccentric in its pursuit of nothing, an implement of confusion and dismay.

Moving near her, Albert held out his two hands, rigid as if drawn against a substance that would lie between them. But she was not looking at him, and in the same moment she turned and walked to the ledge. Arms akimbo, she gazed at the hill where Destina moved; for it was, could be only, Destina. Picking her way among the rocks and scrub in a gentle weaving line.

Fury drawled to derision, as Nadine reviled the moment, the vision, the man, in a harlequinade of verbiage.

'Poetic melancholy!' she cried. 'Complete with moonlight and middle distance. And irrelevant! Oh, what a waste! You're a waster of nights.'

Albert came toward her, hands out, his face sad, moving slowly. 'I told you,' he said in a pleading whisper, 'I said you must not – Why can't you—'

'Oh, now look! She's up at the top of that rock. She'll fall or disappear over the other side. I'm going to call to her.'

'You are mistaken! You are madly, pathetically mistaken.'

'Just the same, I'm going to call to her. Besides,' she added lightly, 'I'm curious. Maybe it's only a ghost.' And Nadine raised her head and shaped her mouth to call out.

But no sound came. Swift and quiet and hard, Albert's hand came across her face. She arched back in the grip of his other arm, her eyes rolling, as he held her body away from him in a sagging curve, shoulders wrenching in the vise of his arm.

'Why won't you understand?' he begged, trancelike, sad. 'I've already said it. No, you can't, you must not make noise.'

Nadine's nails dug into his arm, her other hand flayed the air, trying to reach his face. Against his palm her lips were pressed back sideways over her teeth. Once, straining and pushing, her foot shuffled from the rock's edge into space and the startled body hung over the chasm, kicking like an animal in a sack. Albert pulled her back.

'Please be quiet,' he pleaded. 'Promise you'll be quiet.'

Slowly she stiffened, stopped struggling. She raised her hand in the gesture of an oath. Under the pressure of his palm her mouth bubbled a subdued sound. Very gently then he took away his hand. Nadine spoke:

'Now let me go.'

Albert released her and moved away. She stood swaying, breathing hard, running her fingers through her hair. She was quiet, but stood with head hanging, looking up at him through forward-fallen hair, her entire pose a frown. He was turned again to the opposite hill and its white figure, paused at the crest. When Nadine sprang at him he turned to face her. He saw her swung hand, its intended impact, stepped back. And then with a little whisking sound he dropped away. Like the nimble amazement of the trap door, instantaneous, muffled in shock, he vanished. And moonlight filled the sovereign space where he had been standing.

Lunging against the vacant air, Nadine caught herself

and dropped to her knees on the rim, hands spread flat in the dust. Like an echo of reproach her ears still registered his gasp and the two dull thuds that confirmed his falling. She knelt on all fours, abruptly and finally alone in the pale silence, listening for some further sound. The void withdrew – it seemed to watch her from a distance.

For the first time in her life she was aware of nature. It wasn't at all the nature she had always coveted, it was something else: a cruel, laughing force extravagantly beyond her notions and, above all, indifferent to her existence. All around her in this stony vastness were energetic signs of shared life. From the smallest red ant, the scorpion under his rock, all the quick and the slow, the furtive, the patient, the gentle, the pitiless, the hungry; she heard them now beating on her innermost being, this nature that looked at her with the same disdain that she had shown toward her Hollywood rooms. From disdain the way to hatred is not far, and Nadine was suddenly aware of nature as hostile. She who had never provoked anything but love and adulation was afraid of something she couldn't name. She would not know that to get to the lion was a long journey leading from the louse on the leaf's underside through all the creatures of earth's mastery; nor that a pair of binoculars, far from helping to find him, is an offense to creation.

Across her vision dipped a bird form, a black flutter of wings cawing in its flight a shrill cry. It was so sudden and so loud. Crawling on the ledge she listened as the sound gave way to its own echo brushing the cliffs, the well of the canyon, and the place where only a moment before had been Albert.

Then she screamed and wildly listened as her scream danced back in overlapping echoes. And now another sound came, low and near, a thin groan.

'Albert!' Leaning far out she looked down.

Some twenty feet below, against the wall's face, Albert Exodus clings to a small projection in the rock. His head lies back on one shoulder, his eyes closed, his body hanging by his hands and by a protruding stump of one of those gnarled junipers indigenous to the canyon. The stump has ripped through his abdomen and impaled him, deep under the cage of his ribs. From the wound his blood pours, soaking down through clothes and boots, and a tight coil of intestine, darkly glistening, bulges from behind the torn shirt.

Nadine's frenzied calling fell unheeded. 'Albert, Albert! Are you all right?' She leaned farther, screaming down at his closed face, 'Oh Albert ... Can you ... Albert ... ' Her voice trailed off in a plaintive whine.

Behind his closed lids Albert's sight burned in a quiescent, final lucidity. He was aware of the mutilation of his body as one contemplates the pieces of a porcelain that cannot be mended, wistfully and regretfully, yet with recognition of a completed catastrophe. He felt the stealthy slipping away of his entrails, the busy flowing of his blood as an event, momentous and authentic. His hands were already numb. They would not hold on for long.

Pain would not let him answer the girl, whimpering and frantic on her ledge, for it was all hers now. 'Please say something, Albert! Please, please . . . Tell me you can hang on, I'll get help somehow. Endurance. Hang on, Albert, hang on, for God's sake. Oh, please, Albert, just say something, something . . . '

Endurance, Albert. Hang on. The thought flickered in his brain. But why? Endurance is a barbaric ornament; hanging on a useless metaphor – if he clings a moment more to the rock it is not to prolong life. With an effort he tried again to turn his head, only a little, a trifle, so that his sight might rest on the hill.

'Destina!'

Nadine heard the word. Was it some kind of a name? She pulled her hair at the temples, pulled it taut. Then she picked up a stone and beat with it on the rock floor. Her pale eyes probed the rift. She called again, her voice a ragged banner reaching down in frantic wisps.

'Albert? Are you still there? Oh Christ, what a mess!'

Albert didn't hear. He strained once more to turn his head to the hill, in vain. And then he didn't try any more. A kind of relief held him. There were no more questions, no more words, even for pain. Indifferent now, he waited, his face brushed by the very hairs of death, his eyes and brain ready to burst in a final spray of lightless stars. He murmured over and over the name.

The girl screamed again. 'Albert! Oh, what is he talking about? Destina, Destina . . . What does it mean?'

Finally she couldn't see him at all. Quietly he dropped away, and from the hollow that received him came nothing but a staccato dribble of falling gravel.

Nadine rose to her feet; she went on whispering and arguing with the silence. 'I didn't even touch him. He did it himself, like he did everything. Ignoring me for that kid over there on the ridge – that's insolent – without telling me why – no, that's not what I mean. He just stepped back too far.' She looked across the rift. 'I'll call to her anyway, better than nothing.'

But the little figure wasn't there any more.

'I might have known it. *Merde!* He wouldn't let me call. But why? Is that how it started, this awful crazy mess? Albert. Where is he now?' She began brushing and pulling at her shirt. 'I'm a sight!' Useless thoughts kept tumbling on, useless questions to which she didn't really expect answers: how far to the bottom, how long would it take. She took her comb from a shirt pocket and combed her hair with energy.

'I've got to get out of here somehow. If I can just get back to the horses—' Stumbling, crawling, she started back along the cliff, holding close to its cold face. Poor Albert, that was all a ruse about the lion. Trying to do something extravagant. Oh well, maybe he wasn't. Did he really meant it? She stopped and looked around her as though interrupted, wary, not quite fearful. 'Is he dead? How awful!' Her foot struck a jagged fissure. 'Oh, my toe! Oh-h-h ...' Holding her foot in her two hands she sank down, rocking back and forth, 'My poor toe! I'll never get back to those damned horses, ah, I'll never—'

Stub your toe on a stumbling stone and cry. There's no harm done.

Her face to the sky, eyes screwed shut, she rocked back and forth. 'Destina. What's Destina? What does it mean? Is it a name? Of course it's a name. When I get back I'll ask *him*.' Getting up she tried the foot. 'It's not too bad. Anyway, what can I do? I've got to go on. There's moonlight at least. And it better stay. If I hurry.'

Up and down, in and out of a crevasse, a path, a salt pit, a sandy hollow, steering clear of thorny scrub, running, breathless, half talking, half crying, 'What a farce! Lions! *He* said there weren't any lions here, I should have listened to *him* instead of running out on him like that. Poor Albert. He was all right in his way. He just didn't know what I want.' Plunging ahead, she tripped and fell face-down against the crimson dust. For several minutes she lay there motionless as if in deliberate pause. Then she rose.

A mild wind had come up, laden with blowing sand. She swayed in the gusts, hearing the pulsing of her heart, pulling at her shirt stuck with cactus needles.

Shake the sand from your hair and pluck the cactus spine from your breast. Laugh and say it isn't true. But in the red chasm you'll not have time to cry out.

'Oh no!' she whispered, her mouth open, scarcely moving. 'No, it's something else, something I don't believe.' Then suddenly matter-of-fact, 'No, no, no, it's just too theatrical, the gypsy's curse, how stupid, like a spook movie.' She tried to laugh, but the sound was thin and died inside her.

Giddy and shaken, she went on, head bowed as one who meditates a ponderous and baffling intention. She lurched and often fell, yet rose each time in a kind of numb, determined immunity, her body seemingly impervious to hurt. She talked incessantly to herself. How idiotic, she argued, that she had no gun. When Albert fell the gun went with him. One should not really be in such a place unarmed – not that there was likely to be any need. Not that a gun would get her back any faster to Windcote . . .

When the moon wavered and drew finally behind its pall of clouds she did not notice, aware only of a bleak intensification of misery. Sifting down into her consciousness like some seductive nepenthe came the lure to cry. To give up, yield to wave on wave of awful, flooding despair. But such was not her 'style', she would have said, and indeed she did not falter, still rich in the depravity of hope, still possessed of that shocking, fervid energy often displayed by inexact persons in the presence of disaster.

In a darkness made more opaque by recent light she took a wrong turning and found herself down in a narrow crevice. There was no way out except by the way she had come. She stopped there in bewilderment, her hands lying along the cliff wall. She leaned into the snag of stone, quiet at last, vastly alone, in a sad density of loneliness, eyes closed and without thought. A curious languor prevented her from moving, an acrid stillness wrought of sand and stone pervaded the niche where she leaned.

She felt heavy and even sleepy. From somewhere a question nagged at the tight fit of her self-confidence: 'Where is this current from? Why can't I just go on?

And for a long time the answer gazed back, two holes of sulphur glowing on the furred dark, waking her softly, softly.

Her eyes opened in a throb of recognition to meet the long, topaz stare. She smelled the savage reek, and to herself, 'I guess I knew it would be this way. I guess I've known it for a while.'

Pale-coated in easy pose, he stood just above her, his enormous body swung at right angle to the head as if he would give her the conscious, classic attitude of his kind, so often carved, so rarely understood. He was so near, they too in sudden encounter, she actually felt an impulse to say something, one ought to say *something*, something winning, polite, placative. I'm a friend of Albert, Albert Exodus. He knew you were here, he brought me to meet you. No, no, I can't say that. Albert is dead, and this beast, he knows it all. He has seen everything, watched us. Like the old woman. She knew, she knew! But how could anybody . . . predict? And why, why?'

The animal waited. His yellow gaze fused with her own and ignited the last wing of hope. He seemed to want her to understand. He waited patiently, like a teacher who waits for the toiling child to solve a problem. Then he turned to move, to step down to her. Nadine whirled away. Like a trapped bird smashing itself on a pane of glass she spun around in the dark and flung herself against the rock mass, where a jagged point seemed to be waiting like a knife for contact. Her head struck, she swayed, her arms stretched forward in a blind gesture, she sank down. No sound came. She lay on her side, one arm twisted under her. A red gash oozed and darkened on her temple. Her eyes sparkled like aquamarine in the moon's glow.

He came on slowly and stood over the quiet form, his great head lifted as if in solicitous watchfulness. For a while he did not seem to be aware of the figure under him but looked steadily into the spaces of the dark. Then he bent down, raised his paw and began to tear at the face. Soon he finished, moved away, and disappeared behind the ledge. The body of Nadine lay as it had fallen: the white shirt white; the breeches neatly fawn colored; the varnished nails on pale slender fingers of a hand lying over her heart. But there was no longer a face.

11

When Destina rode out from the canyon's western pass and crossed the gulch that separated mesa from cliff, the first layer of dawn lay on the landscape like a bandage, soaking up the dark, as, hours before, night had blotted out the day. She was not alone. Beside her and a little behind walked her friend. His glide was all rhythm – of easy, multiply moving pads, proudly conscious of sinew, meek in the poetry of that rarest affinity, beast and human. As they passed through shadows the child turned to look back at the cliffs. So rose-soft and sweetly shaped at noon, their pinnacles reared now in grave detachment like histories of old blood, still heavy with night's pall, still guarding their cavernous mysteries: ancient mysteries, mysteries newborn and the ones that have died and live again, mysteries forged in magma and scarred by flood; mysteries so tenuous the very stones cleave in bafflement. Yet, spread before her gaze their fastnesses offered not terror but complicity and containment.

Child and animal came to the mesa's rim. Hills and canyon lay behind, withdrawn and indifferent to the quickening light. A waking bird frayed the air with its caws, and then, with the sound of hooves tapping on stone, the red mare came up. Destina stopped and turned, laid her hand on the lion's head, her face grave.

'Goodbye, goodbye!' But in the next moment she dropped down and threw her arms around his great neck. 'I'm going now,' she whispered, 'back there.'

The little mare waited, munching at the brush. At last Destina rose, grasped the pommel and swung up into the saddle. From her arm hung the handbag. She turned once more to her friend, only looking at him, saying nothing. Then at her sign the horse swerved, she slapped it lightly on the rump, and they cantered out across the dunes. A strong wind had moved in from the west, sweeping sand and tumbleweed in her path. She closed her eyes. Then remembered something. One hand holding the bridle, the other reached into the handbag and brought out a small round object. Bringing it up before her face, her head on one side, she smiled. 'It's so pretty! And blue, pale blue.'

Day was now authentically there, with a relentless sun promising orange heat over all. Arriving at Windcote Destina reined in under the stable portico.

'Jose! You there, Jose?'

When he came out, buttoning his shirt, he hardly

looked at her. She handed him the bridle. To her question – was anybody up? – his eyes stared with a kind of appeal, but he couldn't get a word out, though he seemed to be trying. He pointed to the house, to the upper windows.

'What is it?' Destina asked. 'What's the matter with you?' Oh, he was so stupid. She didn't wait, but ran to a back door and disappeared.

It would be another scorcher, Jose would have said on any other morning. Today he didn't notice, thinking, while he unsaddled Destina's horse, of what Felipe had come out wild-eyed to tell him only an hour ago. He was shaken, but not just by the sheer drama of the event. After all, violence and sudden death were as familiar to him as chili beans or the lack of them. Any Jose, by the time his whiskers grew, had seen enough murdered corpses and spilled blood to think of it all as something virtually unavoidable. Everyone he knew had a dead brother or cousin or father wrapped in their violent story like a winding sheet. That was life – or death. Or life *and* death. 'You'd think they were in love.' That's what his wife Carmela said.

If Jose was pondering what Felipe had told him, it wasn't with horror but with consternation. A fresh corpse might, alas, be your cousin. But if it was your boss, that was something else. It was the end of your job and your pay. No more handsomely paid errands, no more secret deliveries. In fact, he *had* asked about them one day, but only that once – the package had been so heavy.

'Soap bubbles,' drawled his boss, 'butterfly wings. And breakable. So don't drop them.'

These butterfly wings, well, they were made in the laboratory, Nelly had told him. In the part of the lab she hadn't seen. No one had. Very private. And to Jose's crazy question, her answer was, 'Why should any of us butt in? Everybody has secrets and reasons for them. He says so.' That Nelly! Besides, Jose already had plenty of worries: his wife was pregnant again, his girl-friend was pregnant again, and two horses had been stolen from the stable since he went to bed last night. It was a dark day despite the blinding sun. That Nelly! Oh, he could kill her!

12

Coming in and hiding her new treasure in a jar, Destina then went to her bed and climbed in. She would be there when the breakfast tray came. She slept a long time, waking finally with the weight of an unbreathable closeness in the room. The fans had not been turned on. There was no breakfast tray on the little alcove table. An eerie sense of something unusual, like a held breath, seeped into her consciousness of the room, the air, the midday hour. Only the quiet wasn't quiet, as from somewhere she heard strong voices and the slamming of car doors, a very strange combination of sounds for Windcote, especially in the hours of noon heat when everything always waited for late afternoon and its angled sun. She went to a window. There lay the same dunes and, wavering behind them, the familiar boulders and beyond them the canyon itself, all shimmering like water boiling under the noon blaze. Still those sounds. They went on, footsteps going and coming, scraping of moving – furniture? – slamming doors inside and out, then a scream. Not of fear but of fury.

Maybe if she ran to the other room, if she looked out from the other side, where there was a window overlooking the main entrance. Down below three dust-covered ranger cars were parked before Windcote's twin stairs. One of them, a kind of closed truck, back end open, was receiving just at that moment a long black plastic covered burden. It was being slid in by four strange men, all khaki-clad like that forest ranger who had stopped sometimes to ask for water. What was it that was so heavy? What things were these strangers taking away from there? Another man appeared with a big camera. Destina, at her window, watched as he folded it all up and put it in one of the cars.

It was so hot. Two women, that Carmela and her daughter, were bringing water in big pitchers, and there was Felipe pouring it into a radiator. They all seemed to bounce in the heat, hurrying to finish what they were doing. But what *were* they doing? Then the strangest of all appeared: Nelly, elaborately escorted by two very big men, came out, and with their careful help, got into a windowless car. She was led to it rather firmly, with big hands under her elbows, and though she didn't stumble it seemed to Destina that she moved with more than her usual clumsiness.

So Nelly had planned to leave! Nelly with secrets of her own! Here she was, escorted like a queen, with three cars and such a lot of belongings in a big truck. How like Nelly, to not say a word about it to me! Or did Papa know? Was Papa in on this?

It was all very opaque to Destina, leaning on the windowsill. 'Some day,' she told herself, 'I'll leave too. I'll pack up my memory boxes and then go pick up my friend in the canyon and we'll ride in the Land Rover all the way to Albert's house.'

She watched the busy scene below, as they closed the car doors, turned in the gravel and drove away, churning up clouds of dust beyond the gate. That Nelly! If she were gone for good who would bring the trays, who would comb the tangles, who would teach her useless things?

Hungry and baffled as she was, Destina found her slippers, changed her nightie for a pinafore and left the room. A cottony quiet ran along the corridors, engulfed the little girl, and brought her up at the head of the big hall staircase. She stopped there, so that, looking down, banister, marble steps and faraway hall all seemed to gain a portentous dimension, a space that had never before come alive as it was doing now. All those other comings and goings lifted away into a barely believable past, some great height from which she was now floating down, a feather that must ineluctably come to rest on the ground. Of course she would not have been able to express these things; nor would it have occurred to her to describe something so sensory. But a voice inside her said that she was turning into another Destina, one who wouldn't hesitate at the top or the bottom of a flight of steps, anywhere, ever.

She was so hungry by now that the sight of an old woman wearing a sort of hat and sitting in her Papa's great chair at the dining-room table aroused nothing more than a sense of relief. It was, after all, a somebody, a person who could possibly explain this layered puzzle, and who might even help find her some breakfast – though it was, in truth, past lunchtime.

'I'm hungry.'

'Of course you are, my poor darling,' said the aged person, so easy in the big chair and so obviously in charge.

Destina looked hard at her. 'I'm not your darling.'

With a calm smile the baroness reached out to uncover a small tray furnished with what must have been the child's usual breakfast. 'It's cocoa, that you like. And juice, and buttered muffin.'

Completely bewildered, Destina nevertheless eyed the tray. 'All right,' she said in her smallest voice, and putting her hand out to the muffin, 'but I'm not your darling.'

In some gradual and obscure way the questions that had nearly burnt her lips only half an hour ago were becoming hard to remember. Conscious of being as naturally here in the dining room as anywhere else in the world, aware of her table companion as an unwavering presence, she drank her cocoa. And while she ate, the baroness was telling her things in a quaver that gave to the words an almost liquid emanation as of dew collecting into drops of iridescence on her eyes, on her ears, on her mind. 'That was the time when we all thought . . . ' she heard her say somewhere . . .

'When we thought that a dream was something you have at night when you go to bed, and your eyes see nothing but white dust when they open, and it is over. And your ears remember white notes and tremors, because there is no sound in that kind of a dream. That would have been easy to deal with, black and white. No, it was a green dream then, where a woman or a man might slip down and fall in the slimy verdure, the green slitted eyes turned on you with the greenest fire there is, that righteous fire hanging in the doorway and pasted on your windows. They watched her burn . . . '

'Who burned? Who burned?'

'Ours, yours and mine. They used the word. Witch. "You do not write signs," they said, "unless you are a witch."'

'A witch?' asked Destina.

'It was their word. They took her belt and shoes. But you rode away while they watched the flames and raised their hysterical voices to sing green poison. You were seven years old, and when they looked around for you it was too late. As the years vanished one by one and ten by ten you began our journey, you found us our carts, our wagons, our trains, our boats, our silvery cars, our horses; and we moved over the earth before the wind that brought us here. Here is where I saw it all, here in our own incomparable space. I had been far enough, long enough . . .'

Destina gazed wonderingly at her companion. In the high-backed chair she had the look of someone who had always been there. Chair, walls, windows, all seemed to hold her close, to bend to her, even to bow to this presence so long absent. And now to receive her.

' . . . long enough to grow new ears for this desert's thundering whispers and new eyes for the place that had called us back. Here my woeful memories were soon burnt away in the sun – oh, it was good riddance – the title, the shiny jewels, the villas so empty of joy, the many faces with their pampered bodies. Here, we came and here we roamed our domain as the pumas roam, me and my seven-year-old darling on her pony, which grew with her and was soon a horse, a fine horse walking slowly home one day years later, riderless, its bridle hanging, a note pinned to the saddle blanket, a note tattooed on my heart:

'"Dear, dear Mama, I have to see for myself. But I'll come back." And underneath another hand: "Forgive us, Desta, but, knowing you, it is the only way. Her father wants her. To see the life she was born to. Civilized life, if you'll permit me. You no longer want to know us. And so I suppose we do not know you. A. von F."

'They had lured her away, back to the villas and the faces. Years later, one of them found her there: ah, she was the young woman who owned a desert, who had a tiny baby and a broken heart, and who was even grateful for the mockery of this marriage. But it was he who then crept into the land without her while I roamed alone, waiting for her to come back, waiting in vain, for she did not come to save me from the evil that had cast its spell over our world and that had laid this house in the sand like a mockery. Eight years ago he brought into it her own darling, your mother, caught like a songless bird one day on a villa's balcony in that far off place where he found her waiting for you.'

At first all this was too much for Destina's comprehension. She would not have understood that she was the last in a long line of Destinas, that the baroness was her great grandmother and that Papa was not *her* papa. Yet the old woman's voice and its words pleased her. It was a moment full of images, shiny meteors spinning in the air of the room while its ceiling was borne up into a limitless space, while the floor shifted like the sand outside as she, Destina, who might have been asking a thousand questions, was not having the merest thought of Meridian, the papa of this tale. Nor was she thinking of Nelly, who had gone away in the big van and left her, just as Albert had gone, kind Albert, but so far away. She had, it might be said, awakened from some trance, lifelong until now. Had she left one dream only to advance into another? The epiphanic clarity that had seized her only an hour before at the top of a flight of steps was authentic and lasting. It had presaged another reality and a new friend. One day she would ask, 'Who are you?' She did not ask it now.

'He had no use for her, with her belly and her glooming eyes. It was Felipe who sometimes came down to where I was to tell me. I tried to see her. Even when you were born I had no entry. Nor when she died. "An old hag," he told his caller, the one with the briefcase and the papers spread out with ribbons and seals, "claiming kinship, of all things! We shall be kind. We shall not ask for more than the signature." They came down to me where I was, there by Manzanita Wash. They brought smiles and caviar, but I did not sign. He laughed and said it didn't matter anyway, it was for your mother to do. Oh, she signed whatever it was, signed and turned to the wall. I was not told until long afterward. Meanwhile my queries were met with evasion and silence. But I waited. I had to. Waiting had become my way of life. I did it well, even serenely.'

'Sereeny?'

'Serenely. It means without worry. It was enough just knowing you were there.' She would have added, 'my darling', but no, it could wait.

Destina looked again at her companion. 'Why do you wear a hat?'

'I put it on the day your mother died. I've worn it ever since.'

'But why?'

'Yes, ever since that dark day. I made a vow then. I vowed I would wear it until you took it off.'

Destina frowned, ate the rest of her muffin. For a long time that seemed not to exist, they stayed at the table, woman and child, in a golden ambience as the afternoon deepened and waned. Then:

'Come!' said the baroness. She stood up and took Destina's hand. 'Let's look outside.'

In the doorway they gazed at a sky of colored scarves that merged with sierras flowing away on all sides, profiled on the horizon. Long shadows already cast themselves on everything: the clumps of sage, sandy hillocks, the gates of Windcote.

'Now if you like we can go ask Carmela for some ice tea and cookies. Then we'll come out after supper and I'll tell you about the stars.'

The little girl looked up then. 'But first let me take off your hat.'

Leaning, the woman bowed her head as Destina reached out with both hands. The ceremony – for such it was – passed in a moment. For the woman it was like a crowning, in reverse, the lifting of a weight with no name. As for Destina, nothing could seem more natural. Her matter-of-fact gesture, removing the hat, was as foregone as her dawning understanding of those stories, stories that all her life she had in some way been waiting to hear:

'A long time ago when she—'

'Oh, who was she?'

'Your ancestor, and the others who came after. You and me. And your grandmother and your mother. Because he said—'

'Who was that—?'

'Tray Thomas. Tray Thomas said the baby would be a Destina, that we who came after would always be Destinas. He loved her so much. All of us from then on. A long time ago. So we are his, too. We are Thomases. We are Destina Thomas just as she was.'

By the next afternoon much had become clear in Destina's seven-year-old mind. It was so easy. Easy to say 'Granny', easy to view the future without a 'papa' who had never been quite real in any case. And so much better to be tucked into bed by a granny than by Nelly, who had not been very nice. She wondered if she should tell Granny about her friend.

But there would be plenty of time to confide in Granny. For the next few weeks Windcote was hectic, with interruptions and daily visitors, questionings, searches, photographers, even film cameras. They came in official-looking cars, the first ones flashing red lights on their roofs, the men in uniforms with matching caps. They wanted to know about the ugly discoveries out in the mountains: the carcasses of two horses found in the canyon just inside the first gorge, hanging by bridles tied to rock projections, their bellies swollen, clawed open and swarming with flies. Pursuing the trail, a posse of rangers soon came upon the grisly sight of what had once been a girl. As they neared, several crows flapped up from the gaping body, circling as if to show they had got there first.

There was no one to ask, no one to identify the discovery, unrecognizable as it was to begin with. Back at the stable, Jose, quaking with terror, gave garbled accounts of a young man asking for the boss's girlfriend. But since then there was no boss. This mere fact had apparently deprived him of his few words of English, and an interpreter was brought in, quite uselessly as it turned out.

It was the old prospector, doggedly panning for gold deep in the canyon's floor, who had stumbled on the remains of Albert, incomprehensibly wedged in a crevice where the sun never penetrated. These were mysteries to preoccupy the authorities, but not Granny. Although her position on the property was known to them since many years, there were still questions.

Granny dealt with them all. Patiently and with quiet authority she leaned with them over the papers they brought. When they finally went away, apparently satisfied with their findings, she hugged Destina:

'Now, my darling—'

'Now what, Granny?'

'We'll leave now. Today. Tomorrow. We'll go down to our real house, there where I waited for you to come back. It's our home. There are trees down there and birds, not in cages but in the trees and on the wind . . .'

It was late afternoon, almost cool. From where they stood on the terrace they watched the last car whirl in the drive and raise its cloud of dust as it bumped away down the road. Then it was quiet, quiet as it had not been for a long time – even the aviary was silent. Destina's gaze moved across the burnish and purple of dunes, and she heard their singing, deep and secret like the farther crags, the canyon she knew so well. She wondered again if she should tell granny about her friend. The other, seeming to read her thought, added:

'We'll bring your horse. You can roam, just as your own grandmother roamed all her young life before they took her.'

Destina might have asked 'Who? Who took her?' but she was thinking. 'Maybe I won't tell her about my friend. Not just now. Later, maybe, but not now. Not yet.'

In any case there was little time for further confidences. The transfer of Destina's belongings down to the old house occupied them for the next several days, even though there was little of a personal kind in the rooms that had been her home so far. As to her 'memory box', its contents had dried to a uniform black. There seemed nothing for it but to be dropped in the bin with Nelly's clothes and phonograph records. Most of their attention was for the outside: Destina's little mare was there to be attended to, and Granny made arrangements for the aviary birds to be sent down to their Costa Rican forests.

Late one evening, Destina led her horse out of the corral, mounted, and rode to the canyon. There she tethered the horse and wandered her familiar cliffs – in vain. Her friend did not appear. Another night and the same solitary vigil told her he had gone away. She sat on the edge of a deep crevice, dangling her feet over the void. Without her friend, being here among these stones was as unnatural as being at the bottom of the sea. It was, she knew, the end of something. A memory, even an unreliable one. Looking up, she saw it: a piece of dream broken off the rock of herself. There it was, one disappearing spark like a little diamond spun up into the profundities.

She began the descent to her tethered mare. Untying its bridle, she paused for a moment, her gaze on the rolling dunes beyond. Clearly now, there was no reason to tell anything. There was nothing left to tell.

THE MAGIC TOYSHOP
Angela Carter

'This crazy world whirled about her, men and women dwarfed by toys and puppets, where even the birds were mechanical and the few human figures went masked ... She was in the night again, and the doll was herself'

One night Melanie walks through the garden in her mother's wedding dress. The next morning, her world is shattered. Forced to leave her childhood home, she is sent to London to live with relatives she has never met: gentle Aunt Margaret, mute since her wedding day; and her brothers, Francie and Finn. Brooding over all is Uncle Philip, who loves only the puppets he creates in his workshop, which are life-size – and uncannily lifelike.

'She was, among other things, a quirky, original and baroque stylist ... her vocabulary a mix of finely tuned phrase, luscious adjective, witty aphorism, and hearty up-theirs vulgarity'
MARGARET ATWOOD

'Angela Carter was a great writer ... a real one-off, nothing like her on the planet'
SALMAN RUSHDIE